IN THE GARDEN OF LIGHT AND SHADOW

WAR OF THE FALLEN

CERECE RENNIE MURPHY

In the Garden of Light and Shadow: War of the Fallen

by Cerece Rennie Murphy

Copyright © 2025 by Cerece Rennie Murphy

All rights reserved.

Paperback ISBN: 979-8-9913855-3-4

Ebook ISBN: 979-8-9913855-2-7

Hardback: 979-8-9913855-4-1

Cover Illustration: Jocelyn Short

Paperback Cover Design: Jesse Hayes, Anansi Hayes Media

Hardback (Special Edition) Cover Design: Jesse Hayes, Anansi Hayes

LionSky
PUBLISHING

To those who know that evil is a choice, not a destiny,
and fight for the coming of the dawn.
May we continue to stand for what is right.
May we never lose sight of what right is.

PROLOGUE

SABINE

The cold was a good enough reason for Sabine's tears. The wind had been vengeful all day, slicing through the wool of her heavy overcoat and stockings like gossamer blades. It had borne witness to her treachery on nearly every coast so that no matter how Sabine cried, it would not forgive her.

She gripped the edges of her hood a little tighter. "At least Odu has the letter," she murmured. She didn't know where in the world Lilavois was, but Lilavois always told her to keep her older sister Charmaine's address, in case of emergencies, and Sabine had done so. With any luck, Lilavois would get her letter in time to undo some of the damage she'd caused.

Odu Massa was an old admirer of hers from the days when she was still an E'gida in training at the convent in North Kesar and he was the post office's newest apprentice.

On the weekends, she, Jhonna and the other members of the E'gida would go into town to buy sweets and feed on the local gossip. They would often run into Odu at the local tavern as he took his lunch between delivering parcels. Eager to hold her attention, he'd ply them with stories of unusual packages from far off places. He knew whose brother sent notes every week and who had the finest cloths in the world, who moved in and out of town, and who was sending scented messages to a forbidden love.

Some years later, they reconnected after Odu was promoted to Post Office Inspector at the Bevel train station. Though her assignments required constant travel, Sabine always looked for Odu whenever she was in town, if for no other reason than to seek out the familiar affection of an old flame made harmless by time and distance.

A true creature of habit, Sabine found Odu taking his afternoon tea at the same café near the train station where she'd encountered him before, which suited her purpose well. She couldn't risk being seen at the post office. As she placed the letter in Odu's hand and asked him to post it, she knew the message inside was as safe as she could make it. It would survive even if she didn't.

The walk back to the convent was slow and biting, in part because it was the last place she wanted to be. Yet Sabine had no other home. Her family had been killed long ago, and the friends she'd made had all fallen away in her pursuit of an ambition that had led her into madness.

You should have known, she thought, massaging the skin on her forehead against the mind-numbing cold. *Lilavois would have known.*

The convent was nearly deserted when she returned. Most students were away for the midterm break. Others were still in town socializing with the locals or fancying themselves keeping the town safe from the Stone Killer. After dropping off the supplies of herbs and groceries the cook requested, Sabine hurried to her room to carry out the final stage of her plan. With her and her letter safely parted, all Sabine needed now was to disappear.

She'd packed most of what she could the night before. All she needed now was to collect her toiletries and leave. Sabine had no idea where she was headed. For the first time in almost a year she wouldn't be off on some terrible errand.

She would be aimless.

She would be free.

With her small suitcase neatly tucked under the bed to thwart prying eyes, Sabine turned toward the washbowl to gather her toothbrush and hairpins. Underneath the blue cloak of the Sisterhood, she'd already changed into her traveling clothes.

Looking at herself in the hanging mirror above the basin, Sabine found her reflection almost unrecognizable. Her eyes held so much regret their brown seemed almost gray, hovering over a mouth that hadn't seen enough joy to be graced with laugh lines. The once warm glow of her copper brown cheeks was now sallow and faded seemed fitting. Her unlined face looked dry and brittle like a mask.

Still, Sabine was alive, and that was something. With her train leaving within the hour, she had no time left to lament.

She'd just begun fastening the straps on her bag when a shadow at the corner of her eye shifted. Sabine turned and gasped, dropping her bag and its contents onto the floor.

Before her eyes, the shadow grew from a sliver of darkness to a cauldron of black and gray smoke that rose to the ceiling and expanded out.

Fear ignited within her as she ran toward the door, wanting nothing, seeking nothing but to live. She knew she wouldn't escape, but life demanded she try. She did not make it far before the darkness eclipsed all light and something like hot razors cut into her back.

Sabine screamed until she could feel nothing as her body crashed to the ground. Unable to move or feel anything but the blood on her face, she lay there until something grabbed her and flipped her over. Smoke surrounded her. She had just enough air to breathe, but not enough will to scream for help. Even if she could, there was no one who could save her. This fate was hers and hers alone.

"Who have you told?"

Sabine stumbled through her mind to find where she'd made a mistake as the numbness spread through her body.

"I smelled your scent on my things. My ancient things."

The shadow whispered in a voice that was almost soothing. "To whom have you told my secret?"

"I would never betray you," Sabine sobbed.

The darkness pressed in until she was consumed.

"Never," the shadow replied, "is a longer time than you have."

CHAPTER ONE

A BIGGER TABLE

Wild moonflower vines tangled underneath Ada's fingers. For so long, she thought this path, this garden, had been a dream, a delusion of longing and loss.

The scent of lilacs, tea roses, and jasmine filled the air, calling all her long-buried memories forth.

RaZiel's voice behind her was quiet, yet the sound flooded her nerves with sensations of joy and visions of laughter.

"The last time we walked this path together, you were three years old."

She turned, nodded, smiled—hoping that her face conveyed the crowd of emotions that swelled too deeply inside her to give them words.

Besides, they were not alone. Whether hidden in

treetops, gliding above, or perched atop the turrets of their small castle, Ada felt the prickle of two dozen angel eyes silently studying them. From somewhere within the castle walls, she knew her best friend Simon would be watching over her as well. Him, she didn't mind. Yet Ada refused to break the sacredness of the moment by acknowledging any of them.

RaZiel followed from a good ten feet away as she walked down the path, as if to give her space, as if she might be afraid. Ada shook her head at the ridiculousness of the notion. Though his presence was still new to her, the feeling it brought, like the scent of their garden, was achingly familiar.

Before RaHabel, when was the last time she'd heard his voice? Ada wondered.

Memory brought her back to soft blankets and the smooth wood of the inside of a barrel.

"Lie down, Ada. Cover your eyes," he'd told her. At the time, she obeyed him without question. It was the last time her heart was completely free of worry. The last time she truly felt safe.

Halfway up the path that led back to their home, she turned to face him. "For so long, I thought I imagined this place, our time together. What do you remember?"

RaZiel drew closer. "Every blade of grass that bent beneath your feet. Every particle of light on your head."

Ada held out her hand. "Then walk with me, Papa."

RaZiel took his daughter's hand and drew her close,

feeling the familiar warmth that he'd missed so dearly. All around, he heard the gasps of his kin, still in disbelief at Ada's existence. But their burden was not his. RaZiel felt only joy as he placed a kiss at her temple.

"What would you like me to tell you?" he whispered into the curls of her hair.

"Everything you remember. Everything I've missed. Where you've been and how they found you." She paused, trying to control the emotion in her voice. "I have felt your absence all my life. Having you here...I finally get to fill those spaces."

Unlike Ada, RaZiel had no hope of containing his tears. Her absence had been a chasm inside him. Now that they were reunited, it would close—but he knew the memory of the pain would stay with him forever.

"It is the same for me," he whispered.

With her hand in his, RaZiel led Ada to the tree where she was born, recounting the story of his and Lilavois's intimate joy and wonder at creating a miracle—something that had never existed before. From there, they walked to the back of the castle to wander through vegetables and flowers they'd planted when Ada was a child, and they marveled at how many still thrived despite their prolonged neglect. They took their time wandering through all of Ada's favorite hiding places until, finally, they sat down on the grass near the wheelbarrow in the field where their life together had ended, listening, laughing and crying for hours undisturbed.

✹ ✹ ✹

Watching them from the kitchen window, Lilavois felt the ragged edges of her own life stitch back together. Her time with RaZiel since leaving RaHabel had been brief but utterly healing. Though they needed more time alone, Lilavois had no doubt that they would find it. To have him back, to reunite RaZiel and her child after believing she would never see them together again—it was more than she could have ever hoped for. But she knew she could bear the joy of it because she had suffered the pain.

Behind her, SeKet walked into the kitchen, placing the groceries from the market on the table before moving quietly to Lilavois's side.

"We have seen many miracles throughout our existence," SeKet sighed. "But never this. We feel her with all our senses, and yet many still can't believe she's real."

Lilavois smiled, leaving SeKet to continue her vigil at the window.

"You should have been here the day Ada was born," she replied. "The sky itself, and every plant and animal nearby, seemed to rise up to greet her."

"RaZiel said he'd never witnessed anything more beautiful. He told me you lived here together for three years."

"We did."

"He spoke of this place with such reverence. After The Fall, I thought he would never be himself again." SeKet turned from the window. "You have changed him completely."

"We changed each other."

SeKet reached out, taking both of Lilavois's hands into her own.

"You saved my brother. I am forever in your debt."

"You saved us both in RaHabel. It is I who am in your debt."

"Does that make us both debtors?" SeKet joked.

"No," Lilavois replied. "It makes us family."

Together, they organized the groceries they would need for the evening meal in a comfortable silence that turned heavy when Lilavois noticed SeKet shifting on silent feet as she washed vegetables at the sink.

Lilavois had not known SeKet long but instinctively understood that a demon born before the beginning of time was not prone to fidgeting. She put the knife down on the chopping board where she had been slicing carrots and waited.

SeKet looked up from her work to meet Lilavois's gaze with a sad smile.

"I know we only arrived early this morning and this place means so much to you," SeKet began. "I understand, after all you've been through, the need—the desire—to linger."

"I know we can't stay here."

They each took a moment, letting the hard truth settle between them.

"Rah knows you deserve it," SeKet continued. "My brother's light glows as if he were in the midst of the Ever. Looking at him, I can almost imagine we're home." SeKet cleared the longing from her throat. "It has been a very long time since any of us have seen him so...at peace."

Lilavois glanced toward the window. "This is how I know him best. When we were together here. The memory of our happiness is how we survived."

"This is true of my kin as well. Knowing what is possible, having felt it—it's the only thing that kept us sane. Those of us who have forgotten, well, you've seen what that has done. More than Ada's powers, Obi fears the pain of the hope she represents. He can no longer bear it." SeKet did not bother wiping the tears that clung to her chin and cheeks. "He will not stop until he destroys her—even if it means killing our one chance to return."

"I saw the look in his eyes when he tortured RaZiel. I believe every word he said," Lilavois replied with a shudder. "Besides, we need to get Simon back to his family—and warn Liren of what may be to come. Obi's followers know where we lived. It will be the first place they search for us. Everland will surely be the second."

SeKet turned to face Lilavois fully, relieved to see that she appreciated the danger they faced. "Rest assured, Obi will not attack without a plan. The Covenant has also grown in members. Ada is not defenseless." A sly smile spread across SeKet's regal features. "And your association with the Sisterhood will also give them pause. Obi's faction will need time to formulate an appropriate response to the threat we pose."

"What do you mean?" Though her own stomach was in knots, Lilavois was glad to see the shrewd confidence in SeKet's eyes.

"Obi has two problems. The Fallen have never faced open war with each other. That in itself has already divided us. He will have to justify it, but he can't admit who or what Ada truly is because the truth will not help his cause. Quite the opposite. Many will take the chance Ada provides, if only to gain freedom from the misery of our mistake."

Lilavois frowned. "At RaHabel, the reaction to Ada was far from welcoming."

"Sometimes it's hard to accept the truth even if you want to believe it. Our kind have not dared to hope for many years. It will take time to believe again. But when they do, the source of Obi's power will be broken. His determination to move swiftly will be tempered by his understanding of the risks—which will buy us a little time."

Lilavois needed so much more than a little, but for now, she would take what she could get.

Though she dreaded the answer, she needed to know: "How long do you think we have?"

"At least long enough to eat this feast you insisted we shop for," SeKet teased.

Lilavois looked at the bounty of vegetables and meats laid out on the table and grinned.

"It was RaZiel's idea. He's quite the cook."

"I hope so. We bought enough food to feed every angel in the Ever. We had to split up in our purchasing to avoid drawing too much attention to ourselves."

"We've never had so many people at the house. It was always just the three of us. We ate in the kitchen."

"When RaZiel described this place, he told me there was a dining room. For the price, I had no idea what a good investment he made."

"He should have called it a dining hall," Lilavois laughed. "I couldn't believe it when he brought me here. I suppose I have you to thank for his grand gesture."

"Not at all. I merely supplied the funds. In 3,000 years, RaZiel had never asked to buy a single thing." SeKet's eyes shifted to the window as her brother and his child walked back toward the main house hand in hand.

"Perhaps he knew, even then, that one day your family would grow, and he'd need a bigger table."

✵ ✵ ✵

While Lilavois and SeKet led the effort to dust and clean every surface in their home, RaZiel, with help from Ada, Simon, and the other members of the Covenant, prepared a feast. They sat together, twenty-nine in all, enjoying breads and pies, hearty stews, and roasted vegetables—one of the best meals many of them had ever tasted. Yet the food was still only an accompaniment to the stories that flowed across the table like the sweet lavender lemonade they drank. RaZiel and Lilavois recounted the tale of how their courtship began, the life they'd lived together, and the life they'd lived apart.

Seated across from her father, who held her mother tightly as Lilavois snuggled into RaZiel's lap, Ada soaked it all in—every word, every glance, every half-forgotten place— until her happiness was restored. Some stories she'd heard before; most she had not. But with Simon seated beside her, she felt them all, as if she were stitching her life together from threads she had never known were missing.

Most of the questions centered on Ada and Lilavois. The demons were curious about everything—from Ada's powers to the Sisterhood of the Light to how this girl, born of a demon and a human, could exist at all. Simon and Ada chimed in with questions of their own about who the Covenant had been before The Fall, what they had lost, and what they still hoped for.

Though it went unspoken, everyone reveled in the moment because it was fleeting. Their laughter drowned out the rumbling truth that their celebration was only a brief respite from the war that would greet them when morning came.

⚙ ⚙ ⚙

At RaHabel, the amphitheater had long since emptied, but Obi sat at his council seat, unmoved.

His stomach cramped with hunger. The need for sustenance was almost crippling. Stronger still was his resentment, his hatred of needing anything at all. He stared upward, through the hole in the ceiling that SeKet and the Covenant had blown open. The moon was new, but stars shone defiantly through the rupture, mocking him.

Obi sprang from his seat and began to pace. SeKet had come with four angels and left with twenty more.

Seduced by the child, he thought bitterly.

He had tried to tell them she was an illusion, a lie, a new embodiment of God's punishment—an impossible child born of false hope.

But when SeKet and RaZiel flew away, they took certainty with them. In their absence, Obi tried to explain away the events they'd all witnessed as a cruel joke, a betrayal of their right to rule. Few met his gaze. Most disbanded before nightfall, claiming the need for time to reflect until all that remained was doubt and the peace etched into Persephone's very human corpse.

"'Traitor," he spat at her lifeless body. If he could not hold his own flock, what hope remained for their rule? They were permanent beings. Dominion was theirs—payment for being exiled to a world built to die.

Wasn't it? The question jarred him.

"Too much time among the humans," he grumbled to himself. "Their weakness has infected you. Get a hold of yourself."

"Or maybe it's you."

Obi whirled around to find a young man crouching beside Persephone's corpse. He looked no more than twenty, dressed in fine leather shoes, linen trousers and a dress shirt. His ash blonde hair was combed and pomaded in a neat part that had the effect of making him look guileless and innocent except for the crimson coating the tips of his claws as he dragged them though the blood-streaked stone beneath Persephone.

"Lucifer, how dare you come here?"

Lucifer shrugged. "There was no one to stop me."

Obi's indignation dissolved into silence.

Lucifer took his time inspecting Persephone before standing up and turning to Obi. "I heard what happened to Saisho, but I still don't understand." He shook his head. "Persephone looks human."

Obi flinched. "RaZiel has had a child with an E'gida. A child with the power to kill us. Worse—to turn us human."

"That's not possible." Lucifer gestured toward the body at his feet. "That would mean she has the power to grant a soul."

"SeKet believes that God has made the child a soul portal."

Lucifer froze as a fresh sensation of ancient pain lanced through his body.

"How could Nyame have done this after all this time." Tears welled in his eyes. "A child born of the Sisterhood."

"It could be some new form of mooncraft the Sisterhood has developed," Obi replied. "RaZiel and his witch insist—"

"The Sisterhood does not possess this power," Lucifer interrupted.

"Then what?"

Lucifer took a deep, shuddering breath. When he spoke, he was himself again. "Does it matter? The child—whatever she is—must be eliminated."

Obi exhaled. Finally, someone who understood.

"I would like nothing more," he said. "But she is protected. By SeKet and the Covenant."

"How many?"

"Two dozen. I fear more may follow."

Lucifer nodded. "Then we'll draw them out."

"How?" Obi asked, rattled by Lucifer's sudden calm.

"Strategy was never your talent," Lucifer said with a cold smile. "Just be ready when I call."

CHAPTER TWO

ASHES

They gave themselves one night to celebrate, to laugh, to make love, to discover, to rest and revel in the miracle of being together. In the morning, they woke with sober purpose. At dawn, over a simple breakfast of last night's bread and fresh eggs, SeKet confirmed their worst fears.

"Ever since Lucifer was banished, Obi and the council have held our kin together. But now, because of Ada, he faces an unprecedented challenge to his rule. Not only is her existence a beacon of hope to the Fallen, but what she can do offers a path that has never been open to us, one of redemption. The Covenant has broken with him to pursue that path, and many more will come once they've had a chance to process the possibility."

Simon raised his hand.

"You're not in school, Simon," Lilavois teased. "You may speak freely."

Beside him, Ada poked his side and smiled.

"Right," he said bashfully. "I still don't understand why he would deny her at all."

"Obi, and many of my kin, have spent a lifetime as the ultimate authority in this realm. They left the Ever to become such," SeKet replied. "Even with all the pain it has caused us, they would not so easily admit defeat or submit themselves to Rah once more."

RaZiel stood at the end of the kitchen counter, holding Lilavois in front of him, close enough to feel her heartbeat through his skin.

"If he can't get to us, we know what he will do," Al-Yah, one of the newest members of the Covenant, added.

SeKet nodded sadly. "He will do what he has always done: attack the innocent to draw us out and solidify his rule through fear."

Al-Yah frowned. "He could be anywhere."

Lilavois looked to Ada, then Simon beside her. "He'll start where he found us, which is why we're headed to Liren first."

With the ability to transform into creatures large and swift enough to carry humans, the Covenant, along with Lilavois,

Ada, and Simon, arrived in Liren at dusk—just in time to see smoke bellowing up from the burning buildings below. And with the smoke came screams, rippling through the air like sirens.

As soon as their feet touched the ground, SeKet ordered Lilavois, Simon, and Ada to be set down outside the town gates while the Covenant searched Liren for any remaining threats.

Before SeKet could leave, Ada grabbed her hand. "I can help."

SeKet's expression was severe, but kind. "This is not my decision to make, little one. You must speak with your parents."

Without another word, SeKet left to catch up with the rest of the Covenant, who were already beyond the gates, leaving RaZiel to address his daughter alone.

The instinct to protect her was all-consuming, but Ada was far from the little girl he knew from so many years ago. She'd just saved his life two days ago, yet that did nothing to assuage his fear as he faced her.

"You can do more than help," he admitted quietly. "But I would ask you to stay. The scent of my kin is heavy. If one of them escapes us, your mother and Simon will need protection."

Ada saw the truth in his words but couldn't help feeling there was more to it than what he shared.

Her shoulders slumped as she sighed. "I'll wait here until

one of you returns."

"Thank you!" RaZiel hugged her tightly.

His body was so much larger than hers that being wrapped up in his arms felt like being covered in night— peaceful, dark, and so quiet.

"Thank you," he whispered again before stepping back.

Ada watched him transform into a crow, then fly toward the flames.

"That was generous of you," Lilavois said gently. "I wish you'd go that easy on me! I would have gotten an earful."

Ada shook her head. "I think he needed that." She turned to Simon and followed the direction of his gaze into the smoke and flames ahead of them.

"Do you think your father's back from his trip?"

"No, he'll be gone for another two weeks at least. It's my Aunt Belle I'm worried about."

Silently, they reached for each other's hands, looked toward the flames, and hoped.

Twenty minutes later, the Covenant returned. While they reported many injuries, there were no casualties.

Lilavois frowned. "No demon poison?"

RaZiel shook his head. "No. But they did leave messages —with many messengers—so their intent would not be missed."

"What do you mean?"

"The demons who terrorized the town are gone. You can see for yourself."

✿ ✿ ✿

The town of Liren was renowned throughout the provinces for its tranquility. Until the tragic killing of Miles Kipling, there had never been a single murder. But as Lilavois walked among the burnt-out dwellings and debris-filled streets today, it was hard to believe any of that.

The demons had terrorized the town with a cruel but clear goal—to make the cost of harboring Lilavois and Ada so unbearable no one would be willing to pay it. From the burning of the school to the destruction of businesses and homes, the devastation touched every member of the small community that had welcomed Lilavois and her child with open arms. Only the library and the post office remained untouched.

After surveying the damage, Lilavois worked with the town midwife, Ms. Ballard, to organize the effort to convert the ground floor of the library into a triage center. While Ada went to retrieve whatever supplies were usable from her apothecary, Lilavois sent the Covenant to salvage clean linens, wash basins, beds, and whatever else they could from the businesses and homes that had not been burned.

But as the Covenant combed the streets, gathering supplies and searching for survivors, everyone who saw them cowered, ran away, or shrank back into their homes.

SeKet had seen this response before. Given the terror the residents of Liren had just suffered at the hands of demons, the Covenant knew they had every reason to fear their presence. After delivering the needed supplies to Lilavois, they resolved to keep their direct interactions to a minimum.

Without the Covenant's presence, people were less afraid to step out of their homes and help. After bringing the medicines Lilavois needed to the library, Ada and Simon joined a group of uninjured, able-bodied neighbors who had formed a rescue party to inspect every home and ensure every resident was accounted for and receiving whatever aid they could provide. The injured came in by the dozens with broken bones, bruises, and other injuries.

But that was not the worst of the damage.

When asked to recount what happened when the demons came, the story on every tongue was the same.

"They asked only for Ada," Headmistress Mwaso offered, a broken cadence to her commanding voice. "They claimed she had killed one of their own. But how could she? How could I believe it? I've known Ada since she was a little girl. When I refused to tell them anything about her, they burned the school."

"They said Lilavois and Ada were demons. They said they were the reason our son Miles was killed," Mr. Kipling said. "I don't know what to believe. We've never done anything to anyone. How could this happen?"

But it was Lieutenant Fenton who showed Lilavois how

thoroughly the demons had taken the sanctuary of her home away.

"They said if any of you—" The lieutenant paused, gritting his teeth as Lilavois bandaged his broken arm. "—came back, if we helped you in any way, they would kill us. All of us. That was their only warning."

"We had to beg them not to burn down the library," he continued. "I'm so sorry, Lilavois. You and Ada cannot stay here."

"I know," she replied, fighting back tears. "We returned to warn you. To protect you, if we could. You know I would never put anyone here in danger."

Lieutenant Fenton reached out his good arm to comfort her before thinking better of it and letting his hand fall back to his bed like dead weight. Instead, he scanned the room. Lilavois followed his gaze, taking in the wary glances and suspicious stares of people she'd known for years as patients and friends.

"Of course," he began, then lowered his voice. "I've carried your secret for years, but now that it's out—now that it's caused such destruction and grief—it will be hard for others to see the truth as I do."

Lilavois flinched, struck by the insinuation that she and her association with the Sisterhood had somehow brought this evil upon them. If, after all their years of friendship, this was how he saw her, she'd never been more grateful that she hadn't revealed the truth about Ada's father.

How quickly they turn against us, she thought. Even though, she couldn't deny that at the root of all this... was her.

Her choices.

Her love.

Her child.

No, Lilavois thought. *I did not cause this.*

She closed her eyes, steeling herself against her own guilt, a room filled with quiet whispers and hard stares, and the inescapable truth that the demons had destroyed much more than buildings. In a single night they'd erased the goodwill and trust Lilavois had spent more than a decade creating. Unlike bricks and mortar, it would not be easily repaired. Even if it could be, Obi had made sure no one would take that path, not anymore. Between the false choice of her and Ada's safety or their survival, their decision was clear.

Lilavois finished wrapping the plaster on Lieutenant Fenton's arm and checked his pulse. It was almost back to normal thanks to the laudanum in his system, which eased the pain of his injuries.

"The hospital in Bonn is twenty miles from here," she said finally. "Though no one has fatal injuries, some wounds may become fatal if left to fester. I wouldn't advise any of you make the journey in your current state. I'll stay as long as it takes to see everyone stabilized. After that, I'm sure with some help, Ms. Ballard can coordinate care on her own. With any luck, we'll be able to leave by morning."

CHAPTER THREE
BAD INFLUENCE

The rescue party found Aunt Belle nearly buried under the collapsed roof of her two-story home. Though she'd saved herself from being crushed by hiding under her large iron-post bed, she'd still lived through the horror of demons beating their wings against her house as they hissed, "Give us the demon spawn and her mother!"

"I don't know them," she'd screamed as the walls buckled and the roof fell in around her until, finally, they left.

When they pulled Simon's aunt from under the bed, she was rigid with fear. Simon was just relieved that she was alive and relatively unharmed.

"Simon!" Aunt Belle gasped, her dusty yet smooth palms gripping both his cheeks. "Thank God, my boy. Oh, thank God. I thought they would kill me. I thought I would never see you or your father again."

"I'm here, Auntie. I was so worried."

Though his aunt was well past sixty and more soft flesh than bone, her grip was strong as she drew him in and held him close.

"I didn't know where you were," she said, her eyes shining with the joy of all her prayers answered. "I feared the worst."

"I've been safe," Simon answered, easing himself from her embrace. "I was with Ada."

Behind them, Ada stood a few feet away to give them a bit of privacy, as she too thanked God for Aunt Belle's safety.

At the mention of Ada's name, Aunt Belle's eyes shifted, narrowing into sharp points. "You," she said suddenly, venom in her voice. "You are the one they're looking for—the one they say is demon spawn. Stay away from my nephew!"

Ada recoiled, confusion and shock etched onto her face.

Simon gripped his aunt's shoulders more tightly, examining her for head injuries. "Auntie Belle, what are you saying?"

"It's her they want. They tried to kill me because of her!"

"Who told you that?"

"The demons who attacked us."

"Aunt Belle, you remember Ada. She's my friend—my best friend. Why would you believe them?"

"Why else would they come?"

"Because they're murderers who are afraid of her—and what she can do."

"I forbid you to see her," Aunt Belle screamed, hysteria creeping into her voice. "You're coming with me on the first airship to Dahomey. You should be with your family until your father returns." As Simon tried to pull away, she tightened her grip. "Think of your father—think of what he would want."

All he could do was stare, bewildered by the quickness with which fear had made her believe a demon over her own flesh and blood.

"Calm yourself, Aunt Belle. I'm here now. No one is going to hurt us. Ada brought the Covenant that saved us from the first demon scourge here to protect us."

His words seemed to calm her—or maybe it was just the exhaustion of surviving. Auntie Belle rose from the floor on unsteady feet and took Simon's hand. He guided her to the team of volunteers who stood by to carry the injured and the elderly.

"That won't stop them," Aunt Belle whispered as Simon and two other neighbors lowered her onto a gurney to carry her to the triage center.

"We can take her from here," Professor Quinlan, one of the rescue volunteers, assured them. "Rejoin the search party. I'll keep her comfortable until you return."

"Listen to me, boy," Aunt Belle said as her hand slipped from his. "Or that girl will get you killed."

Any hope that Ada had not heard his aunt disappeared

with the sight of her rushing past him, out of the ruined house and into the tangle of debris that was Aunt Belle's front yard.

He found Ada in the street with her back to him. She stood in front of a mound of rubble, rummaging through her mother's travel medicine bag. But Simon knew her efforts were a distraction. Ada had known every medicine bottle and tool in that satchel by heart since she was a child.

"Ada?"

"It's fine," she said. But she wouldn't turn, wouldn't look at him. "She might be right, you know. The whole town thinks we brought this down on them. And maybe we did. Maybe we never should have come here."

Simon stepped closer. "You don't believe that any more than I do." Just over Ada's shoulder, he could see her hands grip the handle of the medicine bag.

"Life will be more dangerous for us now. It already is. You could have been killed in RaHabel."

"I could have been killed here."

"No. They left everyone alive so they could spread the fear they live with now."

He stopped directly behind her. He knew she was aware of his presence, yet Ada hadn't looked at him. He reached over her trembling form to lay his steady hand on top of hers.

"Please stop. This isn't your fault."

"But it is," Ada replied in a voice raw with grief. "They're right to blame me. To hate me."

Gently, Simon placed both hands on her shoulders and turned her toward him.

"They don't hate you. They're just afraid, which is exactly what the demons wanted—to make everyone so scared they couldn't think straight. You may be able to kill evil, but you can't control it. *They* chose to do this, not you. You and your mom have been a part of this community for most of your life. Everyone knows how much you've given. They know you would never hurt us."

Ada took a shuddering breath before meeting his gaze. She couldn't hide her tears from him, or the pain of his aunt's words, but she could give him the truth.

"Simon, you should take the airship to Dahomey."

He shook his head, defiant but not the least bit surprised. "I'm staying here. With you. If anything happens—"

"I would protect you?" she scoffed. "Like I did here for your aunt? You don't know what could happen! What if I'm too far away. What if I don't know you're in danger?"

Sometimes, Simon enjoyed seeing Ada a little worked up. Every once in a while, he'd egg her on just to see her hands ball into fists at her sides and her anger run so hot the tip of her nose turned red. She'd get close enough for him to smell the orange blossom oil in her hair and remind him how much taller he was than her. But he wasn't having anything close to that feeling now because she wasn't just angry, she was hurt.

"I was going to say we would protect each other," he

replied. "You look after me, and I'll look after you. Like always."

Ada stared at him in disbelief.

"With your mom, your dad, and the Covenant here, we've never been safer in our lives."

"We've also never been more hunted."

Simon took a deep breath, searching for the courage to say what he really meant. Slowly, he traced his hands from her shoulders to her neck, resting just under the soft curve of her jaw.

"Ada," he said, "I want to be with you. I don't care what we face."

The tenderness in his voice disarmed her anger. Simon's presence had always calmed her, but this was different. More. The feeling went beyond the circumstances they faced, beyond care, beyond friendship.

It had the familiarity of something she'd watched grow inside her, between them, for a long time, waiting until it was suddenly ready to bloom. Ada could see it, shining and steady in his eyes, waiting for her answer.

She wasn't sure if she was ready, but rather than be scared, she felt relieved and a little giddy as a slow smile spread across her face. She brought her right hand to rest on his at her neck.

"Simon," she whispered, "you *like* me like me."

Laughter bubbled up in his chest. "I do. A lot," he

whispered back before his expression turned serious. "Do you like me?"

Ada smiled wider as she shook her head.

"No, Simon. I think I *like* you like you too."

Slowly, they leaned in. Slowly, their lips pressed together. Slowly, they giggled at the electric sensation their touch created. But they didn't stop until they got used to it.

CHAPTER FOUR

INTRUDER

Ada and Simon rejoined the rescue team, checking every house and every business until they were sure each resident was accounted for, and the extent of the damage and plans for repairs were accurately recorded.

When she returned to the triage center, Ada delivered her reports to Lieutenant Fenton and the residents of Liren with care, giving good news when she could and gentle condolences for precious things lost when she could not. She'd expected a certain amount of grief, even anger, but she had not anticipated the sudden wariness in the eyes of those she most wanted to help, the people she'd known all her life. Some classmates and friends refused to even touch her.

Aunt Belle's words came back to her sharp and new. *That girl will get you killed.*

Ada watched Lilavois work tirelessly to heal and comfort those around them, but while the murmurs of gratitude were consistent, the glares of suspicion and resentment were stronger. It didn't help that RaZiel was constantly by her mother's side, with Ms. Ballard flitting nervously about.

With the only other doctor in Liren unable to stand due to a broken leg, Lilavois had no choice but to ask for RaZiel's help. Obi's horde had destroyed half her medical supplies, including some of the equipment she needed to check her patients for internal injuries. RaZiel's heightened senses proved critical to making sure she didn't miss any issues that needed treatment. It also didn't hurt that, through their years of preparing medicines and working together in Everland, RaZiel was the perfect assistant. He knew which medicines and herbs she needed and was more adept than anyone else at getting them. With no one else as capable, resentful or not, the town needed his help.

By mid-evening, the injured were cared for and settled to the point that Ms. Ballard and a few other volunteers could manage them alone, which meant Lilavois could no longer avoid going to her home.

Ada had mentioned the state of the apothecary when she came back from fetching the medicines Lilavois needed.

"This was all we could salvage," Ada said softly, handing her two carpet bags full of bandages, dried herbs, and medicines.

Ada's eyes were red from tears already shed. Lilavois held her daughter tightly in her arms.

"They destroyed everything," Ada cried, her voice trembling with sorrow and rage.

"They took our house."

Lilavois pulled back enough to make sure Ada could see her clear gaze.

"No, they didn't. Everything that matters—everything we need—we already have."

With a watery smile, Ada wiped her tears and returned to the rescue team. At the time, Lilavois's words seemed to be enough to steady Ada. Lilavois only hoped they would be enough for her, too.

Even with RaZiel at her side, the sight of the remains of her home was still jarring. Shattered glass lay everywhere. But rather than being burned out or demolished, her home and apothecary were ransacked, with broken shelves and drawers thrown about in what looked like a vicious frenzy.

Though she had built the house from the ground up, she could not honestly say she was sorry to leave it behind. She and Ada had made a life for themselves in this place. A good life. But for Lilavois, it was always a place that represented the absence of the second half of her heart—a place without RaZiel.

She had not returned for her memories. She'd returned for her weapons and the tools Ada would need to test and master the new magic within her.

They worked in silence, picking through the debris for anything Ada might have missed. They collected half-used vials of medicine, herbs that Lilavois could give Ms. Ballard, and a knapsack of clothes. Ada's prosthetics were destroyed, but her crutches were undamaged. RaZiel loaded them into the wagon that Lilavois kept at the side of the house, then followed her through the back door and into the garden.

They found it shredded to pieces, flower and vegetable beds ripped open as if pulled from the depths of the earth. RaZiel sighed at the wasted roots, while Lilavois stood beside him with trembling hands.

"Why?" Her voice was a whisper.

His fingers reached out and wrapped around hers. "Mooncraft. They hate how it makes your garden grow. The ground, the plants, they respond to you. He hates that God gave you this gift. I'm so sorry."

Lilavois squeezed his hand and stepped back on to the garden path. "Don't apologize," she said. "You would never do this."

A sudden, loud crash came from the workshop, startling them both.

"Demons," she whispered, inching closer and uncoiling the Lasso of El at her waist.

"Human," RaZiel replied.

The front door to the workshop swung on one hinge. RaZiel pushed it open with Lilavois following closely behind. Though the forge was unlit, the two-story structure was filled with light thanks to a large hole in the roof—which made it easy to see the intruder.

"Lieutenant Fenton?" Lilavois called out. "What are you doing here?"

Guilt followed by panic flashed across his face as his eyes darted from Lilavois to RaZiel. Lilavois lowered her lasso and any hope that his trespassing on her property was innocent.

"I'm sorry, Lilavois," he began. "Truly, I am. They said if we could help them find the mooncraft spell you used to kill them, they would spare us when they returned...I thought—"

"You thought you could rifle through the wreckage of my things and take what is not yours?" Her voice shook with barely contained anger. Fear was one thing, but this was betrayal.

"Be reasonable, Lilavois. They said they'd return and kill every one of us if we didn't help them."

His words cleared her of any lingering doubt that this place could ever be her home again.

"There is no spell for what Ada can do," RaZiel replied, unable to keep the disgust he felt for the man at bay. "She is our child. She was born to her gifts."

Lilavois frowned. "Besides, why would you believe them? You know demons can't use mooncraft. Why would a demon want a spell they can't use?"

"I wasn't in a position to ask questions, Lilavois."

Ignoring Lieutenant Fenton, RaZiel turned to Lilavois.

"Perhaps Obi only means to keep you from it—even though he has no use for it himself."

"'They told us we needed to help them find the source of Ada's power."

"And you agreed to put the life of a child in danger?" Lilavois seethed.

"And you would risk us all to save her?" There was no malice in Lieutenant Fenton's voice, only a quiet truth. "Please, Lilavois. We've already lost Miles. You ask too much of us."

Though Lilavois was truly sorry for Miles's death, Lieutenant Fenton was right. The cold truth of it stuck in her throat. She took a quiet look around the room before answering.

"Just allow us a moment of peace to collect our things. That can't be too much to ask."

Resigned, Lieutenant Fenton shifted toward the door, avoiding Lilavois's gaze.

As he left, Lilavois sucked her teeth. "And here I was, trying to figure out how I could leave a few weapons behind to aid you if they returned," she said bitterly.

"Our best weapon will be our ignorance...and your absence," he replied before stepping out the door and leaving them behind.

RaZiel waited until he could hear the man's feet turning down the block.

"I'm sorry."

"Is he far enough away?"

"Yes. He can't hear us."

"Good. There's no need to apologize. They didn't get it."

RaZiel frowned as Lilavois knelt to retrieve a large, discarded book from underneath the workshop's center table.

"They might not be able to steal her gift, but her legacy— my legacy to her—is worth more than they realize."

The moment she lifted it from the ground, he recognized it for what it was.

"Your grimoire. How could they have missed this?"

She handed it to him. When he opened the book, he found the pages empty. RaZiel looked back at her in confusion.

"Smell the pages."

RaZiel sniffed lightly before turning to her in surprise.

Lilavois smiled. "Indigo ink from the black orchids in my garden. Once written, the words fade. Only mooncraft can reveal them. I know the Fallen can't use mooncraft, but I always felt the need to protect the spells I've created."

RaZiel shook his head with pride.

"I've developed a new system of alchemy, combining mooncraft with physical elements from the natural world," Lilavois said. "What the Sisterhood has done with the Lasso of El , I've advanced. The metal in Ada's leg, her weapons, even some sources of wood, I can imbue them with mooncraft and make them stronger, more adaptable. Sometimes strengthening the bonds of physics, like how the weapons in

Ada's leg fuse to her prosthetic effortlessly to conduct or repel energy as she needs it. I even figured out a way to use mooncraft to make things invisible."

"Truly?"

Lilavois nodded, warmed by the wonder in RaZiel's eyes.

"Only Charmaine knows. She owns an airship yard outside Kemet that we've been using to experiment with ships and weapons. I had planned to send word to her that she should send some of our newest weapons to Liren, but it would seem our help is not wanted."

"Even if they wanted our help, you would risk having your work discovered by the Fallen? Or the Sisterhood?"

"Not anymore. If I can't trust them with Ada, I surely would not trust them with this. This is her legacy. It is hers alone to claim."

"But as a child, she couldn't use mooncraft. The magic that protects her has been yours. Has that changed?"

"No. But now she has access to a new kind of magic. If she can learn to use it the way I use mooncraft, then imagine what she can do."

Lilavois traced an Adrinkra symbol over the blank pages of the book. A pulse of blue light flashed from her palm across the pages, just before a dense, frantic script emerged, filling almost every corner of the page with side notes, carefully drawn images and text, all written in indigo.

"This is what I will teach her."

CHAPTER FIVE

OUTKAST

With few possessions to salvage and even fewer to leave behind, Lilavois and Ada walked away from the home they'd made for themselves, the only friends Ada had ever made, and the quiet life that was no more.

Aside from a tearful goodbye from Simon, who promised to meet them as soon as his aunt was settled, no one was sad to see them leave. It was a chilling demonstration of how thoroughly Obi had achieved his goal. The many years Lilavois spent building relationships as she'd tended to and cared for the residents of Liren, Obi had unraveled in less than a day. With evidence of the demons' cruel carnage everywhere, the town had deemed her, not them, the real danger.

Imagine how quickly the fear will spread in places where no one knows us, she thought with a shudder.

Once their wagon was packed, Lilavois made one final stop at the post office, the only other building besides the library that was left unscathed. At the front of the wagon, RaZiel was conspicuous in his disguise as a wizened groundskeeper. But his kin were much more ominous. Some transformed into a murder of crows that perched on nearby branches while others prowled as a pack of wolves, all waiting outside for Lilavois to complete her errand.

The pristine condition of the building was almost jarring given the near destruction of the rest of the town. For a moment, Lilavois smiled, grateful for another intact piece of the Liren she knew.

"I thought Lieutenant Fenton told you to leave," Mrs. Rouse, the post office clerk, said in clipped tones before Lilavois could fully enter the building. As the only customer in the building, there was no mistaking that she was the target of the woman's animosity.

Lilavois placed a note with her telegram message on the counter before motioning toward the door and the unshattered glass windows where her packed wagon, flanked by the members of the Covenant, was clearly visible.

"As you can see, we're packed and ready to go. I just need your assistance in sending this telegram to my sister."

SeKet had offered to deliver the message directly to

Kemet, but Lilavois was not willing to risk Ada's safety by having even one of them separated from the group.

Mrs. Rouse grunted her acknowledgment before reaching for the paper and reading it aloud.

"We've left Liren permanently. It's time to open the chest. I'll send word where to deliver it when able.

"Love, Lilavois."

The middle-aged woman scowled. "What's this chest?"

Lilavois's gaze narrowed. "Excuse me?" Reading the message was necessary for accurate translation. An inquiry as to the telegram's meaning was highly inappropriate.

"You heard me. I want to make sure you're not planning to bring more trouble here—or to any other town for that matter. I've already sent word to Bonn warning them about what happened here."

"That's why they left the post office intact," Lilavois murmured. In the face of Mrs. Rouse's open hostility, there was no reason to try to quiet her suspicions.

"So we could warn people about the trouble you and your daughter brought here," Mrs. Rouse confirmed.

And spread fear, Lilavois thought.

"As I'm sure you know, we're leaving with little more than the clothes on our backs. The chest holds resources Ada and I will need to sustain ourselves while we find a new home."

Mrs. Rouse turned toward the telegraph machine, grunting repeatedly as she tapped out the message.

Lilavois waited just long enough to make sure the

message was sent before leaving her money on the counter and exiting without another word.

✹ ✹ ✹

With the well-appointed hotels of Bonn no longer an option, RaZiel drove the wagon along back roads and through wooded areas looking for a safe place to camp. Though the journey took only a few hours, every inch forward felt like a league away from everything Ada knew toward a world of danger and uncertainty.

"Where are we going?" Ada's voice was uncharacteristically small and frail as she huddled in the back of the wagon with her mother's arms wrapped around her.

To Lilavois, Ada's shoulders felt a little thinner than they had just yesterday. With a heavy sigh, she turned to her child and drew her closer. Ada had stopped even trying to wipe away her tears, and so Lilavois reached out to coddle and soothe the sadness soaking her cheeks—cheeks that no longer resembled the little girl she once was.

Lilavois knew that these physical changes were not purely a result of the last 24 hours. Ada was sixteen years old. These changes had been happening for years now—but the last few days seemed to have accelerated the journey.

Over the past two weeks, Ada discovered the truth about her father, almost lost both her parents, came face to face with every demon in the realm, and discovered that at least half of them wanted to kill her while the others were still undecided. She appeared to accept all of that with unbelievable adaptability. Until Liren.

Lilavois understood the horror of seeing their hometown destroyed. She'd watched Ada's shoulders bend like her own under the weight of the guilt, the sick feeling that maybe this really was her fault.

They had both worked tirelessly to rescue those who had been hurt and to help in any way they could. For Lilavois, her labor and having RaZiel at her side had been all she needed to keep the guilt at bay; for Ada, those things had not been enough. Every adamant reassurance that Lilavois, RaZiel, Simon, or even SeKet offered Ada was undone by the cold, suspicious stares of neighbors, schoolteachers, and classmates. People who Ada had once considered mentors or friends now only wanted her gone.

Lilavois knew the pain of being scorned. She'd chosen it once. Ada had not. In the end, Simon had been her only ally, her only true friend. Leaving him behind had apparently been the last straw.

RaZiel and Lilavois tried to give them privacy as they said their goodbyes. But Lilavois knew the signs, the tears Simon shed freely and Ada held back as she nodded and tried to smile; the paleness of their knuckles as they held hands; and the soft, chaste kiss Ada reached up to give him before shaking her head and walking away.

It was the heartbreak of losing your only true friend—and the sinking fear of losing a love you barely knew existed until it was gone.

"We're not sure where we're going, sweetheart," Lilavois replied finally. "We can't go back to Everland—they'll expect that. We'll find a place to rest for the night, then I'll figure out what to do tomorrow."

"But I promised I'd send Simon a message when we settled so he can find us."

"I know, baby. When we're safe, we can let him know where we are."

Ada looked up to meet her mother's eyes. The agony Lilavois saw there broke her heart.

"What if we'll never be safe?" Ada asked.

"You can't believe that. Even if it seems that way now, you can't give in to those thoughts. Your father and I, the Covenant—we won't let anyone hurt you. All of us will keep you safe. I promise."

"Simon's aunt was right, Mama. They're going to keep coming for us—and hurting everyone in their path to get to us. To get to me."

Lilavois couldn't deny the truth in Ada's words, but she also wouldn't let them stand.

"Then we'll find them first. But before that, we have to become stronger. You need to become stronger."

Lilavois met the confusion in Ada's expression with a gentle smile. Grateful for the momentary distraction, she reached into the satchel at her side and pulled out the grimoire. Ada's eyes widened the moment she recognized it.

"I thought it was destroyed. How did you find it?"

Lilavois opened the book. "They discarded it on the floor—assuming it was empty."

The hand that was not tucked against the warmth of her mother's body reached out to trace the blank pages. Ada knew her mother sometimes used indigo ink when taking notes. Ada had played with it herself as a child.

"But still... I can't conjure mooncraft."

"No, but you've always had access to my magic," Lilavois replied, nodding toward Ada's leg. "I've been thinking—you might not be able to use my spells to conjure mooncraft, but what if you can modify them to access and conjure your own?"

Ada stared at Lilavois, stunned.

"I use the Adinkra symbols of our ancestors to access and channel mooncraft, but you can choose another method, language, or system that feels right to you. Some in the Sisterhood use kanji. Others use movements. Whatever connects you to the earth—or, in your case, your power. I use the Ananse Ntontan symbol to reveal the ink. Do you know it?"

Ada sat up a little. "The spider's web?"

"Yes." Lilavois gave her a cautious smile. If this didn't work, she didn't want Ada to feel she'd failed. "Pull from your own magic and try it."

Having practiced them as a child—as her first written language, in fact—and grown up with the Adinkra symbols all around the house, Ada knew the seven-pronged spindle shape by heart. She traced the symbol over the blank page with a pulse of her own magic, then watched in awe as her mother's words and diagrams bloomed in ink on the page.

Lilavois's smile widened with pride as Ada flipped through the pages of the book greedily. A glimmer of excitement flashed in Ada's eyes. "Does this mean I get my own lasso?"

"Ah, no." Lilavois replied, snuggling closer as Ada lowered her gaze in disappointment. "We're going to focus on you learning how to summon your own source of magic then using it as I've used mine."

"To make ourselves safe." Ada's voice was still weak, but it strained toward hope.

"That's right," Lilavois said. "That's exactly right."

CHAPTER SIX

KIN

By dawn, under the cover of ancient trees, RaZiel found a place to make camp a few miles outside Bonn's city gates. His kin moved forward, surveying the area, while RaZiel and Lilavois began the process of making camp.

While Ada finally got some rest, they surveyed the area. The clearing was big enough to hide their wagon and tent but not much more. With two dozen angels traveling with them, Lilavois doubted there would be enough space, but RaZiel assured her this would not be a problem.

He pulled her close and whispered in her ear, "Don't worry, my love. We will be safe here." His breath in her ear sent a delicious shiver down her spine. "We do not need shelter as you do. The trees will protect us."

It was early morning when they arrived, bright enough

for the light to break through the leaves to the forest floor and cast gold-green patches of light. But as Lilavois turned to look at the stand of trees surrounding them, the light began to fade. She squinted, watching the morning sun obscured behind a thick cover of leaves until only ambient light illuminated the area.

With a gasp, she realized what was happening. Lilavois's gaze darted as she adjusted to the dimming light. "The trees are moving their branches together. For you."

RaZiel pulled her closer, brushing his lips against her cheek. "For us," he corrected.

She closed her eyes and gave in to the heat of his touch. "Ada is close," she said, tightening her grip on his shoulders.

A large crow dropped down to the ground beside them before morphing into the shape of SeKet.

"So are we," she teased.

RaZiel laughed, tucking Lilavois into his body before she could pull away in embarrassment.

"And don't be so impressed," SeKet laughed. "The trees don't only move for him. They have agreed to be our shelter as well. It will be easier to keep watch.

"There is a farm almost two miles away," she continued, "but it will be simple enough to keep an eye on. They're far enough away that they should not bother you. There's a stream nearby for fresh water. Between the provisions you salvaged from Liren and what our kin can forage, you can stay here safely for a while."

Lilavois stepped out of RaZiel's embrace with a frown. "You keep saying 'you.' Why not us?"

Lilavois watched as the smile faded from SeKet's face. "Kibuka and Hina will stay with you, but we must go."

"You hunt Obi," RaZiel replied.

SeKet nodded. "He will not stop with Liren. We must find him and bring others to our side before he spreads more lies, turning every human against us."

Before yesterday, Lilavois would not have believed that people could be turned against them so quickly, but if the people of her own community could be convinced in one night to shun them and choose their common enemy instead, the rest of the world could hardly be expected to do better.

"Where will you go?" Lilavois asked.

"Some of us will start in Everland, while others will begin scouting the other provinces."

"There are too few of you to be safe so scattered," RaZiel warned.

"We have no choice. There are too many lives at stake if we do not. And don't forget—he wants us to find him. He will make his mark terrible enough to reach us. When one of us has found him, we will combine our strength and defeat him."

"Ada could set him free," Lilavois said.

"True. But that will have to be his choice. I would not risk exposing her to those about whom we are uncertain. We go not only to hunt him, but to share the miracle of our redemption." She paused. "But first, we fight."

RaZiel nodded, torn between his fear for the Covenant and his duty to Lilavois and his child. Yet there was no doubt where he would stay.

"I cannot go with you," he said simply.

"No. You cannot." SeKet smiled. "Our greatest task we leave to you, to protect God's gift to us, our one and only path home."

⚙ ⚙ ⚙

Under the watchful eye of RaZiel, Kibuka, and Hina, Lilavois and Ada made good use of their days.

The mornings were reserved for Ada to practice summoning her power and shaping it into a defensive shield she could use to protect herself. Unlike the child she'd had to cajole into getting to school on time every morning, Lilavois found that Ada had no trouble waking up with the birds and the sun now. One morning, Ada even beat her to breakfast.

"My goodness! You're eager," Lilavois teased. "Where was all this early-morning energy before?"

Ada did not smile back as she sipped her tea and ate the last of the stale bread and hard cheese.

"It wasn't a matter of life and death before."

"Ada..."

"If I want to have a normal life, to even have a life, I need to learn my craft. The sooner I do that, the sooner we'll be safe." Ada hesitated. "The sooner I can see Simon again."

Lilavois averted her gaze. She didn't know what lay ahead for them, but as much hope as she had for her daughter, she doubted anything in Ada's life would ever be normal again.

"Your life will be as extraordinary as you are," she said encouragingly. Ada's shoulders drooped down, the exact opposite of what Lilavois had intended. Not willing to risk another misstep in trying to comfort her daughter, she turned her focus toward the task at hand. They ate in silence, finishing their breakfast quickly.

"You ready?" Lilavois said, finishing off the last of her tea.

Ada stood, clear-eyed and determined as she followed her mother deeper into the trees.

Through meditation, Ada discovered that her magic felt like a dormant force inside her, which, now that she recognized it, was easy to call forth. Without focus, it was almost imperceptible, a low hum in the recesses of her mind, but the more she learned to listen, the louder it became.

In the afternoons, Ada studied Lilavois's grimoire, deconstructing and memorizing the techniques she used for combining mooncraft with alchemy. Like her mother, she was fascinated by the art of blending magic with the elements around her—metal, wood, stone. Unlike Lilavois, Ada's magic did not require her to pull from the earth and moon. Instead, Ada shaped her magic through a deep connection to the intention behind how her power would be used.

When fusing that magic to another element or weapon, Ada's familiarity with the Adinkra symbols her mother used proved invaluable. Not only did it help her understand the spells her mother used, but, through Lilavois' example, she created her own shorthand using the sacred Adinkra symbol for reconciliation and hope to represent the intention and purpose of her gift. Unlike her mother, Ada needed no words to summon her power. She only needed to hold the intention of what she wanted in her mind, inscribe the symbol into the object she wished to enchant, then send her power through it. Her challenge was sustaining enough focus to push her magic through the many layers of matter that existed within each item.

Her first successful enchantment was an arrow from her quiver. It took her three days to enchant and gave Ada a new respect for the skill and concentration it had taken her mother to make Ada's prosthetics and the countless other things that her mother made, and she'd taken for granted.

But nighttime was Ada's favorite because after dinner, she and RaZiel would walk.

Under the canopy of willows and elm trees that seemed to shiver and genuflect whenever her father passed, RaZiel would peel back the ordinary and show Ada the world through his eyes, from the far-off gaze of the stars to the low heartbeat of the earth itself. With his patient, soft manner, he slowed the whole world down so that she could finally pay attention.

With no one to compare herself to, Ada had always thought her keen sense of sight and hearing were better than normal—but nothing worth noting—until RaZiel opened her eyes to just how much more her senses could perceive.

Her keen memories of childhood, once dismissed as dreams, revealed the depth of her capacity to memorize and recall details. All of this, she now realized, was far from normal. She'd inherited these gifts, but her father unwrapped them so she could finally see them for what they were.

Most nights, they wandered until the wee hours of the morning, walking through the darkness with perfect clarity while RaZiel shared stories of other worlds and species.

Sometimes, Ada insisted that he draw her a picture of the planets and places he described. Other times, RaZiel simply transformed, bringing to life creatures that no human would ever see.

When she yelped and laughed in surprise, RaZiel could almost imagine that he hadn't lost thirteen precious years—that no time had passed between now and when he'd last heard her wild laugh as a child.

One night, prancing around as a unicorn from the Rishi Maze galaxy, he offered her a ride on his back. With an adamant shake of her head, Ada refused him, instead taking a moment to sit on a fallen tree trunk.

"I think I'll pass on that ride for now and rest a bit."

He morphed back into himself immediately.

"Forgive me. You must be tired. It's very late."

"Not really. It's just my leg."

RaZiel hesitated as Ada parted the split in her skirts and eased her leg out of the prosthetic. In moments like this, RaZiel remembered just how much time they'd lost. His gasp was small, barely an exhale of breath, but of course Ada heard it.

"Is there something I can do to help?" he offered.

Ada shrugged as she began massaging her leg. There were only two people in her life she trusted to touch her leg without pity—her mother and Simon. Could RaZiel be the third? Ada wasn't sure.

"Does it hurt you?" he asked quietly.

"Not usually. Back home I had several prosthetics to choose from. Sometimes it helps to vary them. Plus, the ground is uneven here, which can be a bit more difficult to navigate. I just need to ease the strain on my muscles."

Silently, Ada noted RaZiel's pained expression as he took in the soft folds of flesh that surrounded her severed bone.

"Does it bother you?" she asked finally.

Ada only took her prosthetic off in front of those she trusted, those she considered her family. The memory of RaZiel's words from her childhood had not faded. "Ruined," he'd said. RaZiel was her father, yes, but she needed to know if he was more than that. She needed to know if he was truly her family.

His hesitance pricked at her heart, but she refused to hide

the fullness of who she was from him. If he couldn't handle it, she needed to know now.

RaZiel stepped closer. "No," he replied, sitting down beside her. "It's just... I've never seen it healed. It's hard for me." He slid to his knees.

"May I?" His hands hovered, waiting for her consent.

Ada nodded.

His hands were warm and gentle against her skin. "The last time I saw your leg, you were dying. We had to amputate it. You were bleeding. And now you're whole again, but different."

His hand traced the space where her knee would have been. Where her skin was stitched together.

"I can't look at it and not remember the pain of almost losing you. This is the line between life and death."

Ada watched him until their eyes met.

"Your mother saved your life that night," RaZiel said. "I pray you don't remember it."

"I don't, but Mama said you helped."

"I did what she taught me to do. My kin, we do not change. It was hard for me to understand that you would heal. I'd never had to truly comprehend that before."

"I remember you saying I was ruined."

RaZiel stared at her, confusion etched on his face. "I didn't. I said *I* had ruined our life. Your injury was my fault. I watched your mother heal from your birth, but that was natural. What happened to you was not supposed to happen. I failed you."

"You didn't choose this. I still remember the smell of the blankets as I hid in the wheelbarrow. I remember the sounds of you fighting to protect me. I remember you begging them not to hurt me. This wasn't your fault. Sometimes... bad things happen."

RaZiel did not answer. The truth was still too difficult to sift from the pain.

"Do you still see me differently?" Ada asked.

"I do," RaZiel admitted.

Ada's eyes fell as the hurt pierced her, before RaZiel took her hand and raised her chin.

"When you were little, all I could think about was all the things the injury would take from you, all the things you wouldn't be able to do. But now I see you are more, more than I ever imagined. It is a very human thing to learn and grow from change. Your injury has made you stronger somehow, better than you would have been before. I did not expect that, but I should have. You are our daughter."

CHAPTER SEVEN

NEIGHBOR

For nearly three weeks, they managed to avoid contact with anyone. Kibuka and Hina took turns going into town to gather news and supplies. Disguised as travelers, it was easy for them to slip in and out of Bonn without being noticed.

But on the eighteenth day, their anonymity came to an end.

RaZiel and Ada had just begun their evening walk when they heard the sharp cry of a child followed by a howl of pain more than a mile away. RaZiel raced from their haven to find the child and bring him to Lilavois for treatment.

Despite his injuries, the boy pushed RaZiel away.

"Don't eat me," he whimpered through the pain of a broken arm. "I don't want to be turned to stone."

It was then that RaZiel realized that in his haste to reach the boy he'd forgotten to disguise himself.

"Calm yourself. I will not harm you."

With no hope of running away, the boy opened his mouth to scream until Ada burst through the trees and rushed toward them.

"Help!" he wailed. "He's going to turn me to stone!"

Ada reached them smiling and out of breath. "No, he's not. We came to save you."

The boy's eyes shifted from terror to confusion as he looked between Ada and RaZiel. When he reached for her, she took him carefully in her arms.

"We need to get you back to my mother quicker than I can carry you, but I won't leave you. I promise." Ada glanced up at her father with a sly smile before turning to the boy and asking, "Would you like to ride a unicorn?"

❈ ❈ ❈

With the help of a warm fire, a few drops of laudanum, a soothing voice, and some firm bandaging, the boy was well enough to drink a cup of soup and tell them who he was and where he'd come from within an hour.

"My name is Ephraim," the little boy said around a mouthful of bone broth and carrots. "We live on the farm just past the last bend in the brook."

RaZiel nodded toward Lilavois to confirm that was where he'd found Ephraim.

"And what were you doing in the brook all by yourself?" Lilavois asked.

Ephraim shrugged his thin shoulders. "Just wandering. I meant to catch a fish for dinner. It got away, and I slipped."

"I see." Lilavois smiled, watching him gulp down the last of the soup. "We should get you back to your parents. I'm sure they're worried."

"My mother," Ephraim corrected. "My sister was killed by a demon. Like you," he said, pointing to RaZiel, who stood some distance away from the fire. Ada thought it wise not to mention that two other demons were perched in the trees above them.

"You must be related to Ms. Abbe?" Ada asked, putting together his story with the article she and Simon had read in the Crimson Herald.

The boy frowned.

"I'm sorry for your loss. My friend Simon and I read about her in the paper a few months back," Ada replied, then pointed to RaZiel. "He will not hurt you. He's not like the others."

"How do you know for sure?" Ephraim said, his keen eyes flicking between them.

Ada sensed her mother's tension. But the thought of Ephraim fearing RaZiel, thinking he was like the other demons, broke her heart. Watching RaZiel stand apart from her and her mother after everything they had been through was something Ada could not allow anymore.

"I know because he's my father."

Ada turned toward RaZiel and held out her hand. Cautiously, RaZiel closed the distance between them.

"These are my parents."

Ephraim stared in amazement, as if the answer to a great mystery had finally appeared.

"My mother said that demons can't have babies."

"They can't—normally. I'm the only one," Ada admitted, trying to keep the sadness of this admission from her voice.

"My sister lost her arm, too. What happened to your leg?" Ephraim asked, pointing to the prosthetic and the soft blue glow it emitted.

Ada smiled at his frankness. "When I was little, a demon tried to kill me. My parents saved me. My mother made me a new leg."

"Is that why you're here in the woods?"

Lilavois squeezed Ada's hand, silently urging her not to answer.

"Kind of. It's a long story."

"I like long stories," Ephraim said.

"But I'm sure your mother is very worried about you," Lilavois cut in. "We should take you home."

Ephraim turned to RaZiel. "Will you come too?"

"I'm not sure your mother would be comfortable in my presence."

"My mother always says she likes anyone who is good to her children."

Lilavois smiled. "It is best for your safety—and ours—that as few people as possible know where we are."

"Don't worry," he said. "My mom can keep a secret even better than me."

CHAPTER EIGHT

BONN

Ephraim was true to his word when they arrived at Mrs. Abbe's home. Her shock at finding two strangers and one demon at her door was dampened by her relief at seeing her youngest child safe.

She greeted them in a sweater that had been thrown on backward and boots that were barely laced.

"I just finished searching all his usual hiding places," she said while holding her son. "I was just about to search the forest."

Over Mrs. Abbe's shoulder, Lilavois could see the dinner Ephraim's mother had set on the table, cold and untouched.

"Why do you worry me so?" she cried, rocking him back and forth in her arms before Ephraim winced and pulled away.

It was then that she noticed the splint on Ephraim's arm.

"I slipped in the brook," he rushed to explain. "I know you said it was dangerous, but it's our first Ramadan without Farrah. I wanted to get you a nice fish like she used to. I know... I know you miss her."

Mrs. Abbe's face crumpled as she lifted her eyes to the sky to keep her tears from falling. When she felt back in control of her grief, she looked down at her son.

"You are a good boy, but I do not need fish. I need *you* to come home safely. That is what I need. Okay?"

"Yes, ma'am."

She eyed the strangers at her door, lingering on RaZiel a moment longer before she took her son and stepped aside.

"I'm grateful to you for helping my son. My name is Mira Abbe. Please, come in."

Ephraim shared his dinner with Ada, while Mira ushered RaZiel and Lilavois into the living room.

"Given your daughter's murder, I'm a bit surprised by your welcome," Lilavois began after she and RaZiel accepted the tea Mira offered them. She waited for Mira to take a sip before she drank. Poison wouldn't affect RaZiel, but she still felt it best to be cautious.

"My village in Mir was saved by the Covenant. It was a long time ago, but I remember you," Mira said, nodding to RaZiel. "My husband and I came here to find peace, and we had it for a little while before he died. Regardless of what happened to my daughter, I know that not all demons are evil."

"Thank you," RaZiel offered, leaning forward. "I wish those in Liren felt the same."

"We smelled the smoke a few weeks ago. There are wanted posters for you two in town. Thankfully, I have not seen anything for your daughter. There is speculation... that you are the Stone Killers."

RaZiel had not seen the wanted posters two weeks ago when he disguised himself and went into town. *Obi must be escalating his efforts to find us,* he thought. He had not heard from SeKet since she left; he could only imagine the mayhem she and the others were fighting against.

Lilavois frowned. "We knew they'd sent warnings. That's why we haven't traveled farther. We don't want to bring trouble to innocent people or make ourselves targets for others to bargain with the demons. We were forced to leave Liren."

"I see," Mira said softly. "Well, you're welcome to stay here. I've seen enough to know there is no deal to be made with those who want to rule over us. Only a fool would think so."

"Thank you again. We've made camp a few miles away. So far, we've gone unnoticed. We don't want to cause you trouble," RaZiel added, "or draw undue attention to you. It's safer for you not to associate with us."

"If that were true, my son might still be stuck in the brook with a broken arm—or worse. The least I can do is keep watch and let you know if I hear anything."

❀ ❀ ❀

For the next few weeks, RaZiel, Lilavois, and Ada kept their distance, and Mira kept her word, leaving messages folded under a rock beneath a large tree outside her property.

For a while, the posters and the accusations in the newspapers stayed the same. Though the Covenant fought against Obi and the destruction he wrought, the very people who had benefited from their protection began to see them as the cause of the latest scourge.

But as the weeks drew on and Lilavois and RaZiel remained hidden, the stories and the lies became more desperate.

Usually, Mira did not bring Ephraim to the market with her, but ever since he snuck away and broke his arm, she was loath to have him out of her sight. Traveling to Bonn was rare, yet Mira was efficient, gathering provisions quickly and keeping Ephraim focused with the promise of a small treat from the grocer when they were done.

After loading their supplies from the hardware store, they headed into the grocer to get the herbs that Lilavois said would help with the incessant itching that made it hard for Ephraim to keep his bandages tight enough for his arm to heal properly.

Knowing the store well, Mira gathered her supplies with

haste and moved to the counter. Beside the cash register was a display of assorted candies in five clear jars.

"You can pick *one*," she told Ephraim while handing her basket to the store clerk.

Behind the clerk, Mira noted the curled edges of RaZiel's and Lilavois's wanted posters still pinned to the wall. But that was not what caused her heart to race. Beside them was a new poster of a poor likeness of Ada with the title *Known Accomplice*. The depiction of her was slightly older, with a menacing stare.

"That'll be forty-three decals, ma'am."

When Mira didn't answer, he spoke again. "Ma'am?"

Following her stare, the clerk glanced at the wall behind him and added, "Scary folk, but don't worry. No one's found 'em yet. But they will."

Mira averted her eyes to hide the flush on her face. "Uh, how much did you say?"

Before the clerk could answer, Ephraim stepped up beside her with a peppered caramel candy in his palm.

"That looks nothing like her," he scowled, offended on Ada's behalf.

Mira hushed him immediately. "How would you know?" she laughed, her voice betraying the harsh glare she gave him.

Ephraim blanched as the clerk narrowed his eyes. "What'd he say?"

"I said, how much for the groceries? And add this candy to the total," Mira answered, smiling broadly.

"Oh, that'll be forty-four total," the clerk replied, looking slightly confused.

Mira paid him quickly and hustled out of the store, but she already knew it was too late.

She could feel his eyes watching them as they left, stepped into their wagon, and drove away.

CHAPTER NINE

THE GULLS

They came in the night, which was their first mistake—for what is darkness to a demon?

After rushing home to warn Lilavois, Ada, and RaZiel, Mira prepared. No one asked her to. In fact, Lilavois had begged her and her son to flee, but Mira could not bear to abandon the home she'd built and the burial ground of her husband and daughter, not if there was a chance it could be saved.

After the notoriety of Farrah Abbe's death, everyone knew where she lived. Mira knew what to expect. She'd lived through this before—in another time, another life away from where she was now. She packed their clothing and dried food and sent it all with Ephraim to Lilavois and RaZiel, where she knew her son would be safest.

When they finally arrived, torches in hand, Mira was ready.

"We don't want you," Sheriff Bartlett warned. A posse of twelve heavily armed men rode behind him. "We already sent word to the Fallen. They said they want peace—like before. Things will go back to the way they were as long as you hand them over."

Mira scoffed. "A peace that will only last as long as they want it to? What kind of bargain is that? You're too old to believe in fairy tales, Bartlett."

"Where are they, Mira? Your family and I were friends. After your husband died, I led the search to find Farrah when the demons you're defending put her down. How could you protect them after what they did to your own child?"

"They aren't the ones who killed her. They're the ones standing between us and the Fallen ruling over us forever."

"You're on the wrong side of this, Mira. The Fallen are already on their way. Don't make this harder than it has to be." Bartlett paused. "Don't make us burn through you to get to them."

"There will be no peace once they arrive. In Mir, they destroyed my village. They'll destroy Bonn too, and every town in between."

"She won't tell us on her own," said a man Mira recognized. The grocery store clerk from that morning stood just behind Bartlett. "Besides," the clerk laughed, "if they're such good friends, how come they left you out here on your own?"

With a swing, he threw his torch toward the roof of her house. It did not land.

Catching the torch was child's play from where RaZiel hovered in the shadows over the clay shingles. He lingered only long enough to blow out the torch before launching himself to the ground.

"She's not alone," RaZiel said, landing silently beside Mira.

Bartlett reared back, ready to order an attack, but his words were silenced as Kibuka and Hina descended from the trees and landed in the middle of their posse. The horses bucked and reared, startled by their presence, but Kibuka and Hina calmed them quickly.

"Put down your torches. We mean you no harm," Kibuka said.

"This is an ambush!" one of the riders from the back of the group yelled before turning around and riding away. Two others followed him.

Bartlett tightened the reins of his horse and tried to muster a brave face. "If you mean us no harm, then why have you been hiding in the shadows?"

Hina, who stood in front of Bartlett, tilted her head in confusion.

"We'd hoped making our presence known would be unnecessary, but you came here with your torches to harass this woman and her child. We would not stand by and let you burn down her home."

Bartlett was furious, in part because of the effort it took to keep his own horse from nuzzling up to the demon.

"We're not here for you," the clerk shouted. "We only want the one they call RaZiel and the two witches that travel with him. That's all we want."

"They are innocent of the crimes of which they've been accused," Hina explained. As she stepped closer, the entire posse stepped back. "We cannot give you what you seek."

"Please," another man pleaded. "We don't want to end up like Liren."

Lilavois stepped into the clearing from where she'd been hiding with Ada, crossbow in hand.

"You've already sealed your fate in that regard."

"Did you ever stop to think why a group of demons would hunt their own?" Mira asked.

"They said they were trying to stop the killings," Bartlett stuttered.

"And you believed them?" Lilavois asked. "These are members of the Covenant. They're the ones fighting on every shore to keep the Fallen at bay. And now the demons are using you to get to the Covenant—our only defense. The Fallen have never been trustworthy. Why would you trust them now?"

"They said if we turned you over, they would leave us alone. Like they did in Liren. They said we'd be safe."

Mira shook her head in disgust. "And when every member of the Covenant is dead by their hands, who will stop them from enslaving us? From unleashing another scourge that we will be powerless to stop?"

She stood back, watching the color drain from Bartlett's cheeks as understanding finally took hold.

"But why you?" the clerk said. "Why not the whole Covenant? You must have done something."

RaZiel looked to Lilavois, unsure of what they should share. "It's not what we've done. It's what we can do that they fear," he said finally.

"And what's that?"

"We've discovered a way to send them back permanently. That is why they want us dead," Lilavois replied.

"Oh God," the man in the rear muttered. "We need to get back. We left our families. Will you help us?"

Kibuka closed his eyes and took a deep breath before answering. "We'd better hurry," he said. "Your town is already burning."

CHAPTER TEN

UNWANTED MERCY

Riding on Mira's borrowed horse, Ada and Lilavois kept pace with Bartlett and his posse while RaZiel, Kibuka and Hina kept watch from above. Sitting behind her mother, Ada held on tight, grateful for the warmth of Lilavois' body to press against.

Ada had been to Bonn with her mother and Simon only a few times but remembered it fondly as a bright and bustling place. Two-story buildings with walkways on both floors covered with bright yellow canopies that lined the cobblestone plaza on three sides. Each level hosted a variety of businesses and storefronts, from grocery stores and tailors to butchers and solicitors. While Bonn was much smaller than Kemet, it was still lively compared to the quiet town of Liren, and Ada had always been excited for the chance to visit. For weeks, she'd looked forward to a change of scenery, a chance to experience something other than the forest, but now all she felt was fear.

She'd prepared for this. Every arrow Ada had enchanted was strapped to her back or secured to the saddle. But as she and her mother reached the forest's edge, the smell of smoke grew thick, clinging to the back of her throat and nostrils. The scent, the acute feeling of panic it raised in her belly, reminded her of when they'd touched down in Liren.

Would all her training be enough for what they faced?

Ada dismounted, flanked on either side by her mother and father. In front of her, the vibrant city she once knew was marred by plumes of black smoke and the sight of people fleeing in whatever direction they thought might offer them shelter. Even in the forest, the air was stagnant, casting almost everything in a thick gray ash. The only color she could see clearly was the bright orange of the flames consuming each building in the square, inch by inch.

Obi's demons had wasted no time ravaging the city they promised to protect. They hadn't even waited to confirm whether Sheriff Bartlett had been successful. Then again, that had never been their goal. It was as Lilavois told them, Bonn's fate was sealed the moment its leaders aligned with the Fallen.

Startled and afraid, Bartlett and his posse stood behind Lilavois and the others. What had seemed like a large gathering at Mira's house looked like nothing at all against a demon attack.

Lilavois turned to them, her voice holding a deep anger for what they might cost her and a genuine pity for all they had lost and were about to lose.

"We'll act as a distraction. Kibuka and Hina will go into town first to begin evening our odds and driving people toward the forest. When they arrive here, it will be your job to usher them to whatever safety you can find."

Lilavois didn't wait for Bartlett or anyone else to answer as she passed out the crossbows and arrows that Ada had imbued with her power. The power of each arrow was as extraordinary as it was rare. If the arrows worked as intended, they would have the same effect on each demon as Ada would have been able to deliver with her own hand. If they didn't work, then at least she and Ada would be together for whatever happened next.

There were only fifteen between them. RaZiel took none for himself, while Kibuka, who would go into Bonn first, took five. Hina took two arrows, holding one in each hand like a dagger, leaving four each for Ada and Lilavois.

"Be careful," RaZiel whispered, bringing Kibuka and Hina into a fierce hug.

"Protect Ada," they whispered before folding into shadows that mimicked the gray around them and making their way into the city.

Only Ada could hear their private conversation. Knowing

that Kibuka and Hina were willing to risk eternal death to keep her safe did nothing to soothe the twisting in her stomach. With a deep breath, she tried to refocus her mind away from her fears and toward at least being useful.

As Kibuka and Hina moved through the market square in secret, Ada and her family got into position behind three large trees that would give them the best vantage point from which to strike. The plan was to give Kibuka and Hina as much time as possible to diminish the size of the threat they faced while saving as many people from the demons as they could.

Looking out into the space where Kibuka and Hina had disappeared, Ada tried to see through the plumes of smoke. Even with her exceptional eyesight, the smoke made it hard to take a clear shot at the targets, three men and three demons, who stood on an elevated stone platform at the center of Bonn's market square. It was easy to tell them apart. Only the men in front had claws around their necks.

Ada gasped in recognition. "Those are the men who ran away at Mira's house."

"Yes," Lilavois replied as she loaded a spelled arrow into her crossbow. "They should have stayed with us."

From the platform at the center of the square, where the hostages were on display, the demon, Leophrastos, called out.

"I can smell you in the trees, brother," he taunted. "There is no point in hiding. We know you're here."

"Then release them," RaZiel replied. "They have nothing to do with what is between us."

"They are the bait," Leophrastos laughed. "Got you and your mate and your spawn here, so I'd say they've served their purpose. If you want to save them, like I know you do, come out and exchange your lives for theirs."

RaZiel looked down at Lilavois, who had begun tracing the Akoben Adinkra symbol of a crescent sitting atop three sharp lines into the ground as she chanted. Then he looked over at Ada.

"Do you have a clear shot?" RaZiel asked.

"Not yet. She's working on it," Ada replied.

Between them, Lilavois's fingers hovered above the Adinkra symbol, palms glowing blue as she murmured to herself.

The wind around them picked up—barely enough at first to rattle the leaves or flutter the frill on Ada's cotton blouse. But then Lilavois rose to her feet, and the wind rose with her. A gust of cold air, damp and tinted pale blue, swirled around the ground before spiraling up and pushing toward the town. It came in gusts, one after the other, as it pushed the smoke away and quelled the worst of the raging fires.

Leophrastos squinted against the wind in disgust.

"Do not use your foul craft against us, witch!" he bellowed.

Each demon standing behind a rider closed their claws tighter around their necks. But Lilavois, Ada, and RaZiel didn't need to wait any longer. The smoke was clear, and their targets stood in full view.

"It would be nothing for us to kill them and leave their blood on your hands," Leophrastos shouted. "There are plenty of people to kill here. How many will lose their lives before you surrender is up to you."

The thought of this man, this half-human, half-bear demon that she first met in RaHabel, taunting them, playing games while people suffered, burned her fear into a sharp, focused anger.

You first, Ada thought.

Ada and Lilavois stepped from behind their trees and fired three arrows in quick succession. Bartlett's crew stared in fascination, watching as the arrows shimmered through the air, gathering light with each inch they traveled until they burned like a streak of pure sun. They flew with an unusual quickness and struck each demon exactly as intended, in the soft, vulnerable tissue of their necks.

As the demons stumbled back, gasping in disbelief at the unfamiliar sensation of physical pain, Ada stepped forward, drawn by the evidence of her enchantments taking hold. The two demons on the right shifted into a series of horrific beasts before they finally took human form. Leophrastos made no transformation at all before the wound on his neck began to bleed, pulsing from the arrow that was lodged between his collarbone and chest. Disgust gave way to terror—and then awe—as he fell to his knees and died.

"It worked," Ada whispered, looking between her mother

and father, her face shining with a dawning pride. They smiled back, trying to keep their worry from showing.

For an instant, there was silence, as if each witness had taken a pause to acknowledge the new reality that was open to them—a world where demons could be killed by humans.

And then, with a piercing shriek, calm disintegrated into chaos.

CHAPTER ELEVEN

FOR BETTER OR WORSE

This was the moment Lilavois and RaZiel had planned for—the moment when they found out just how badly they were outnumbered. Lilavois and Ada had worked to imbue every weapon they had with Ada's magic so that every kill would be mercy. But there were only four of them, with too few weapons, and any number of demons standing in the way of Ada's safety.

The sight of three demons killed out in the open spurred a rush of people to come out of hiding. A few stopped and stared. Most ran, not wanting to test the limits of whatever luck or magic had kept them alive.

But above the mayhem, roars of inhuman terror began to rise from different corners of the plaza, and with it came a flood of demons and people pouring out from every doorway.

RaZiel and Lilavois stared in horror as they realized that, though their plan had worked, it would not be enough to save them.

"Tell everyone to take cover in the forest," RaZiel said. "Once they're safe, we'll try to block the path to give people the best chance to escape."

Behind them, Bartlett spoke up. "We're ready. We can help get them away."

"Good. Do that," Lilavois agreed, still finding it hard to forgive how he'd brought this danger upon them.

"There are so many," Ada gasped, shaken by the chaos before her.

Lilavois grabbed Ada's trembling hand and held it tight. "Stay close. Your father and I will protect you, okay?"

Ada nodded, too scared to speak, but her feet moved forward. *No matter what happens*, she told herself, *as long as we're together, this is the safest place to be.*

"Take cover. Head to the forest!" RaZiel ordered, running ahead.

To Ada, stepping into the square felt like diving into chaos, with people running, begging, pushing and falling all around her. They moved as if there was no hope, as if at any moment they could be annihilated by the simple prick of a demon claw.

Ada realized the difference between herself and them all at once. Though she was scared, she was far from defenseless.

A demon had already tried to kill her—and failed. She had an uncommon power within her and was learning to use it more and more every day. While others ran away from demons, she ran toward them because no matter how frightened of them she was, she had something almost no one else in the world could claim.

They were afraid of her, too.

She had power. She had her parents beside her, and just like them, she had not come here to hide. She'd come here to fight.

Ada let go of her mother's hand to fully match their pace.

"To the forest!" she shouted. "Get behind us! Hurry! We're here to protect you!"

Though she kept her eyes on the crowds rushing past, Ada could feel her parents' eyes on her, beaming with pride. For a moment, Ada allowed herself to imagine that maybe, despite all the chaos, most of the town would be able to escape, until she heard a roar from above.

From the second floor, Ada saw two demons snarling and wrestling with each other in a blur of motion. A large pane of glass shattered as they crashed into the storefront window. Ada recognized Kibuka immediately. His crossbow was nowhere Ada could see. The quiver strapped to his back was empty, which told her he'd been successful in using them to reduce the number of demons they would have to face. With no more arrows left, Kibuka's claws came out. Dodging a head-on attack, he raked his claws down the demon's chest, then whirled through the air and out onto the second-floor landing.

"Stay down, Alekwu," Kibuka commanded. "I don't want to kill you."

For a moment, Alekwu was dazed, confused that Kibuka had not used his demon poison to kill him.

"So noble," Alekwu sneered. "After killing five of our kin, you want me to thank you?"

"We don't have to kill innocent people to settle this, Alekwu," Kibuka pleaded. "We can let them go. This fight has never been theirs."

Ignoring his brother, Alekwu focused on the crowd of people below—some frozen in terror, others scrambling to get away. His face twisted into a malicious sneer as he remembered the bargain the Fallen had made, a lesson Lucifer had taught them long ago. If they could not have love, then fear would suffice. Without looking back, Alekwu leapt over the second story veranda. He landed in front of the main support beam, which held up the right corner of the building, then rammed his shoulder against it with the full weight of his rage.

The first crack could barely be heard against the din of frightened screams, but even from across the square the deep cracks radiating from the impact made it clear that Alekwu had hit his mark.

"RaZiel!" Lilavois screamed, tossing her crossbow and

arrows to him so she could continue helping people move through the square.

As he nocked the spelled arrow, RaZiel was aware that he could have crossed the distance to Alekwu almost as fast as Ada's arrow, but he would not leave Lilavois or Ada's side for any reason. The arrow met its mark just as Alekwu crashed into the pillar again, shattering it to pieces.

RaZiel wished him peace, but that was less than half his worries. Above Alekwu, the structure began to crack and buckle.

"Run, Kibuka!" RaZiel screamed. "Run!" But inside, he knew they were the words of a helpless man, wishing there was something he could do.

He watched in horror as Kibuka raced back through the second floor, searching for anyone who might be trapped. He managed to secure one person under each arm as he ran, but there was simply not enough time to save them all.

Kibuka leapt from the balcony as a sharp crack rang through the air. He came down beside RaZiel just in time to see Alekwu buried beneath the rubble he created. The outer walls of the building collapsed first, then folded in with the roof as each storefront crashed down like dominoes, leaving the structure and all those who were too afraid to leave or who were using the building as a place of refuge trapped underneath.

Kibuka looked at the two people he'd brought with him. Though he was no longer holding them, they remained frozen in place, captive to the terror all around them. "Go!" he yelled, finally penetrating their shock enough to send them running without a backward glance.

Kibuka, Lilavois, Ada, and RaZiel formed a tight circle around each other as the chaos grew. Those who could escape the demons ran with renewed urgency, avoiding the shelter of buildings just in case they collapsed too. RaZiel and Ada fired their crossbows, taking down demons with three of the four arrows they had left so as to buy everyone who was able more time to escape.

But underneath the turmoil that surrounded them, Ada could not ignore the cries of those trapped underneath the storefronts.

"There are still people alive in there! We have to help them!"

Lilavois looked to the rubble, heard the screams, and shook her head. "There's no time," she said, as the sound of broken glass and new screams erupted from the left side of the square.

The throng of people shifted, pushing RaZiel, Ada, and Lilavois back as Hina emerged from the first-floor storefront window, towering over the crowd at nearly eight feet tall. She took three steps before shifting into a pale blue bird with white-tipped feathers and taking flight.

A large hulking animal with the torso of a lion and the lower body of a bear chased after her.

"Murderer!" it growled. "Betrayer! You killed them! You

killed them!" The creature launched into the air, claws open
and reaching for Hina's foot. Yet, it could only grasp the tips
of Hina's feathers as she used her wings to climb higher.

"Judah! No!" RaZiel called, but he did not heed.

Furious that Hina had gotten away, Judah reared back,
shifted into a red bird with tight slim feathers, and took flight.
Having transformed into birds that were larger than any on
Earth, their battle could be seen clearly from the ground.
With a vicious fury, Judah chased Hina as she climbed using
his long, curved beak and sharp claws to try to tear her from
the sky. Though Hina was adept at evading his attacks, her
efforts to avoid confrontation only seemed to heighten Judah's
anger.

"Why doesn't Hina fight back?" Ada asked her father.

"She is trying to show mercy, even now. If Hina strikes,
Judah will be lost forever."

They watched as Judah's claws came so close to grazing
Hina's belly that Ada and the others feared she was pierced
through.

"But Judah won't give her the same chance," Ada replied.

Their wings beat against each other so forcefully the
gusts could be felt across the square, until the unmistakable
sound of bone snapping rang out above them. Hina's scream
was deafening as she fell from the sky, one wing flapping
desperately as the other hung limp.

The impact of her body cracked the stone pavement
beneath her. Yet, Judah gave her no time to recover. He

landed on top of her, transforming once more into his half lion-half bear form as he placed one large paw on Hina's broken wing.

"You will die here, as your brethren did, and become nothing," Judah hissed, raising his poison claws to strike.

But Ada had made her choice.

Every demon who chose to leave RaHabel had done so in part because of their desire to return to their home, their creator. She would not deny Hina that chance. Her arrow pierced the soft down of Hina's underbelly before Judah's claw fell. Startled by the flash of golden light, Judah shrank back. Hina's body shifted from a bird to a panther to a woman. Tears fell from her eyes as her body began to bleed. There were no words between them as she died, but the look of gratitude on her face as she turned toward Ada and took her last breath told Ada that Hina understood the sacrifice she'd made.

Ada had used their last arrow.

She was so transfixed by the joy on Hina's face that she did not see Judah lunge toward her. By the time Ada noticed, Judah was dangling just above the ground—pierced through by RaZiel's claws.

"I'm sorry, brother," RaZiel whispered as Judah disintegrated into ash. "Even now, I wish you peace."

Lilavois inched closer to Ada. The chaos of a few moments ago had settled into an eerie quiet. Those who could run had made their way to the forest. Lilavois only hoped Bartlett could see them to safety. Except for the injured who took shelter in a few of the remaining buildings, those who remained had scattered deeper into the city.

It was just as they'd hoped—except now Lilavois, Ada, Kibuka, and RaZiel were in the open and completely exposed.

CHAPTER TWELVE

CHANGELING

"You will not kill another of my kin."

The voice echoed across the square so loudly that at first Lilavois couldn't tell where it was coming from—until a demon she knew well from RaHabel stepped out from one of the storefronts that was still standing.

Vishin came from the opposite end of the square in a pale cream tunic and pants that were pristine despite the destruction and smoke, save for one sharp tear in the fabric that ran across his shoulder and chest.

"You claim to hate violence, yet you wield it so easily now," he mused, coming fully into view.

"This violence is of your making," RaZiel replied. "Our kin died because of you."

Vishin frowned.

"It was necessary to lure you here. If you had surrendered your witch and the child at RaHabel, none of this would have been necessary."

RaZiel stepped in front of Lilavois and Ada, his stomach sickened with the knowledge of all their worst fears confirmed. There was never any peace to be had. The attack on Bonn and all the people needlessly killed there was merely a trap.

"I alone am responsible for my transgressions."

"True. But that's hardly the point now, is it?" Vishin moved his gaze to Kibuka. "Give us the girl and no more lives need be wasted."

Kibuka drew his claws as he shook his head. "Never."

Vishin sighed. "Unfortunate. But expected, I suppose. I must admit I thought this would be simpler. How hard could it be to catch one little girl? But I see now how deeply I've underestimated you, RaZiel. I did not anticipate that the girl's power could be made into weapons." His eyes narrowed.

"I did not imagine we would lose twenty of our own kin at your treacherous hands," Vishin said. "You forced me to pull back and reassess your motives. I brought enough Fallen to destroy every man, woman, and child here. I thought if I killed them one by one, you'd eventually break, but at what cost to my kin? I didn't know how many weapons you had. But then it occurred to me, given your newfound comfort with death, seeing a few dozen humans you don't know killed might be a bit distressing, but commonplace at this point. Perhaps a more personal connection might inspire you to rethink our terms." He paused, smiled. "Luckily, I found just the motivation you need."

With a wave of his hand, two demons emerged from the darkness, each holding a man in his arms. Though they struggled against their captors and wore sackcloth over their heads, Ada didn't need to see their faces to know exactly who they were. Though both men, one older, one younger, had a long, lean build, the younger wore a brown satchel across his torso that Ada would recognize anywhere.

Even before she said the word, her feet were moving. "Simon!"

Lilavois grabbed Ada's arms to hold her back.

Satisfied his plan was already working, Vishin walked over to pull the sackcloths off. Simon's face was smeared with dust and blood from a gash on his cheek, but his eyes burned with anger and defiance as he struggled against the arms that held him. Simon's father, Matthias Abara, had a swollen bruise above his right eye. Dust covered his hair and shoulders. He looked around wildly, fear and shock plain on his face.

"I remember your friend from RaHabel," Vishin cooed. "I thought he would have gone into hiding with you. Imagine our surprise to find him here without you. You're not a very good friend."

The demon who held Simon reached into his pocket and handed Vishin the remnants of an obsidian-tipped blade.

"He did manage to cut me, but..." Vishin waved a hand over the smooth skin under the tear in his shirt. "It's healed now."

Ada couldn't see properly through the tears in her eyes. She'd gone from fighting against her mother's iron hold to shaking with the first true fear she'd felt in weeks.

"Release them!" RaZiel demanded, stepping forward. "They have nothing to do with this."

"You have always been a terrible liar, RaZiel. Though it pleases me to see you try. The child knows exactly what they have to do with this. Give her to us, and they will not be harmed."

"Please," Ada begged, "I'll come with you. Please don't hurt them."

RaZiel looked back at Ada, who was now wrapped fully in her mother's arms, barely restrained.

"I will not give her to you," RaZiel replied. "Take me instead."

Vishin shook his head then turned to Simon and Matthias. Their captors released them, only to shove them to their knees. Once on the ground, they yanked Simon and Matthias back by their hair then set a hand on their right shoulders.

"I would order them killed by our poison," Vishin shrugged, "but that would be too clean."

In response, the demons tightened their grips. Simon and Matthias grunted in pain but refused to scream.

"You know what I want," Vishin said. "I will not ask again."

RaZiel drew his claws. Though he'd never seen the boy's father, he'd known Simon since he was just a little boy trying to defend Ada in the schoolyard. RaZiel knew then that Simon loved her. It was a child's love, but it had grown into a silent vigil in the heart of a young man who would hold in his own pain to spare Ada anguish. If RaZiel could not save Simon's life, he could ensure his murderers would lose their own.

"Kill them!" Vishin shouted as RaZiel bolted forward.

Ada watched as Simon's and his father's heads were yanked back, and heard the tension between skin and bone as the demons began to slowly tear them apart.

"No," Ada screamed as something wild rippled up to the surface from the core of her being.

Without thought, her power unleashed. Breaking the vice of her mother's hold, Ada's arms flew out. Luminescence coursed underneath her skin, turning her brown eyes the color of smelted gold. Light shot out from her fingertips, piercing the demons who held Simon and his father.

They released Simon and Matthias instantly, howling in shock as their bodies transformed.

Lilavois looked up at her daughter. The surge of Ada's

power had knocked her to the ground, yet she could barely see her through the glow of bright light that surrounded her.

Celestial, Lilavois thought with tears in her eyes.

But the light faded almost as suddenly as it appeared. Ada gasped, then faltered. Sensing something wrong, Lilavois scrambled to her feet just in time to catch her daughter as she fell.

CHAPTER THIRTEEN

LAST HOPE

To keep her panic at bay, Lilavois checked Ada's breathing, pulse, and temperature. Ada's body felt light in Lilavois's arms, but she was still alive, which was all that mattered.

The reason why she collapsed, how she'd conjured this new power, and what it meant for her body to unleash such energy were all questions to be answered another time. First, they had to find a way to get her out of here.

"Stop them!" she heard Vishin hiss.

Alarmed, Lilavois looked up, only to find him retreating from the platform, apparently unwilling to risk his life to carry out his own orders.

Rather than chase him, RaZiel and Kibuka focused on cutting the binds from Simon and Matthias's hands and feet. They'd barely had a moment to stand before chaos erupted around them once more, with a new wave of seven demons streaming from the storefront doorway and windows where Vishin had retreated.

"Hurry! They're coming!" Lilavois screamed.

They made it back to her just in time to be surrounded.

When they left camp with their entire supply of fifteen arrows, they'd assumed it would be enough. Surely, they thought, Obi would not send more than fifteen demons to track them. Looking at the demons that formed a menacing circle around them now, it was clear Obi had sent more than twice that many.

Carefully, RaZiel lifted Ada from Lilavois's arms and turned to Simon.

"Are you ready?" he asked.

Simon did not look at him. Instead, his gaze was fixed on Ada's peaceful expression.

"I am," he replied, reaching out to cradle her body against him.

RaZiel watched as Ada turned into Simon's hold, unconsciously nuzzling her cheek against his shoulder. Simon smiled, despite the hopelessness of their situation, and leaned down to kiss her cheek.

"Then may God be with you."

Lilavois, RaZiel, Kibuka, and Matthias formed a tight circle around Simon and Ada. In addition to RaZiel and Kibuka's claws, they only had two daggers and Lilavois's lasso between them, not nearly enough to make a stand, much less survive.

RaZiel leaned down to kiss Lilavois. "I love you," he whispered. "Now and always."

Lilavois looked at him without a trace of fear, eyes shining with only love—only determination to see her family live past this day.

"Always," she whispered back.

RaZiel looked forward, but cast his voice back toward Simon. "On my signal, take her. Run to the forest. Find the horses and don't look back."

CHAPTER FOURTEEN

MESSAGE RECEIVED

From among the circle of demons, Giada stepped forward with a sad determination etched on her face.

"We wanted the girl," she began. "No more. But you've chosen your path. It pains me to know that your life will end, brothers, because of your own choices."

RaZiel and Kibuka said nothing as Giada signaled for the Fallen to proceed. They stepped forward slowly, knowing their captives had no chance of escape, until a sudden gust of wind from above and the muffled sound of propellers stalled their advance.

Giada lifted her gaze to the sky, but found nothing to account for the disturbance—nothing anyone except a member of the E'gida, who knew the shimmer of her own mooncraft by heart, could see. Lilavois gasped in relief as six masks dropped from the sky and landed at their feet.

Hastily, she handed RaZiel her lasso and dagger, then scrambled to pick the masks up. "Put these on. Quickly," she ordered.

"What is this?" Giada demanded.

Ignoring her, RaZiel turned to help put on Simon and Ada's masks. As soon as the last mask was secure, canisters of gas rained down, exploding in front of the Fallen. RaZiel almost felt sorry for them as they began to cough and gag the way he had so long ago. He remembered well the burning of obsidian poison.

The air shifted above them, circling as the gas canisters were followed by a storm of arrows. The demons broke apart as they ran from the moonfire tips that pierced their skin. As their lines broke and scattered, the gust of wind grew closer until Lilavois and the others had to huddle together to withstand the gale.

The vibration of a large, heavy object landing shook the ground until the veil of mooncraft pulled back to reveal the mahogany and bronze visage of the airship Cypher. Lilavois looked up to see Captain Claybourne, Jhonna, and two dozen E'gida race from the vessel, armed with the weapons she had created.

RaZiel and Kibuka spared only a moment for surprise before running to join the E'gida in creating a perimeter that drove the demons back. Lilavois trembled with relief as the demons fled, creating a widening zone of safety around Ada, Simon, and his father. After the last member of the E'gida had emptied the ship, only Charmaine St. James remained, standing at the Cypher's entrance. Her eyes searched the chaos, combing through the bodies and the blood, until she locked eyes with the one person she had traveled so far to find.

CHAPTER FIFTEEN

TRIBE

Lilavois couldn't ever remember seeing her sister run so fast—yet it wasn't fast enough. They met halfway, crashing into each other with wild, grasping arms. After a moment, Lilavois tried to step back, but Charmaine held her closer.

"I feared I would not arrive in time," she whispered.

Her voice held a deep, raw pain Lilavois had never heard before. Reflexively, she squeezed her tighter, breathing in the heady scent of Charmaine's rose perfume, and laughed, tears sliding from the corners of her eyes. The scent was pure rose oil with a hint of freesia, so entirely out of place in the havoc that surrounded them. And yet Charmaine's very presence had been the antidote to the evil that had almost taken their lives.

"You, late? You've never been late a day in your life," Lilavois teased.

Charmaine stepped back and shook her head, smiling through her tears. "I'm just glad today was not that day."

Over Lilavois's shoulder, Charmaine could see Ada leaning heavily into a tall young man.

"Is she hurt?"

Lilavois followed her gaze. "No. Just exhausted from the use of her power."

Charmaine's eyes flashed with alarm, but she kept her questions to herself. "Let's get them to the ship."

With RaZiel, Kibuka, and the members of the E'gida driving the demons back, Charmaine and Lilavois helped Simon, Ada, and Matthias into the Cypher's small but efficient care unit, stocked with a full array of Lilavois's medicines. Captain Claybourne returned to the ship to help Lilavois stitch and treat Simon's and Matthias's cuts and bruises and give Ada a tonic that would quell her dizziness and restore her strength. Though she had regained consciousness, Ada was still too weak to stand on her own. Once the injured were settled and resting, Lilavois and Captain Claybourne tiptoed from the room and closed the door behind them.

"Thank you for coming," Lilavois said quietly as she squeezed his hand in gratitude. "You saved my family."

Captain Claybourne smiled. "It was mostly your sister's doing."

"I'm sure," she smiled back. "But she wouldn't have gotten here this fast without you." When Captain Claybourne began walking back toward the deck, Lilavois followed.

"What's our current situation? I can join you outside—"

"No. You can not," Charmaine interrupted, walking down the aisle toward them with a small tray filled with three biscuits and two cups of tea in her arms. "RaZiel, Kibuka, and the E'gida have already cleared the Fallen from the area. Jhonna has taken command of coordinating the rescue and treatment efforts for the injured who've been left behind, as well as recovery and burial plans for the dead. Captain Claybourne, I believe RaZiel was hoping you'd assist him with the search."

"Of course." Captain Claybourne nodded with a smirk as he left Charmaine to continue ordering her younger sister around. When he was gone, Charmaine continued.

"So, as you see, there is nothing left for you to do but sit down, drink this tea, and tell me what the hell is going on."

Too tired and grateful to argue, Lilavois led them to a booth beside one of the Cypher's large, round windows. To her credit, Charmaine waited sixty whole seconds, enough time for Lilavois to take a few sips of tea and devour half a biscuit.

"Lilavois, what happened to her?" Charmaine asked. "Why does our girl look so frail?"

"Her powers surged while we were fighting the Fallen and I think her body needs time to recover. It's not uncommon among the E'gida for some apprentices to be overwhelmed the first time they summon their shield. In the beginning, it can take time for your body to adjust to the increase in energy flowing through you."

"Did you experience that?"

"Not while I was at the convent, but I saw a few other apprentices go through it. I think... By the time I learned to summon my shield, I had Ada. I was already mature in the use of my mooncraft. It felt natural, almost easy."

Charmaine leaned in and lowered her voice. "Ada's abilities have been growing?"

Lilavois looked around to make sure they were alone before answering.

"They have. Since Liren, we've been working on honing her skills. I've been teaching her my own mooncraft spells and incantations to see if they would work with whatever the source of her power is."

"Did it work?"

Lilavois nodded. "Better than I ever imagined. Ada has learned to merge her power with weaponry. When they strike a demon, it transforms them, just as if she killed them by her own hand."

Charmaine's lips parted in shock.

"This could change everything about how we fight the Fallen. Anyone with a spelled weapon could kill them."

"It already has. By the time you arrived, we'd run out of weapons, but each one we used worked."

"Do you think the process of making the weapons drained her?"

"No. She seemed fine until they brought Simon and Matthias out and threatened to kill them. By then, our weapons were gone, and they were too far away to protect."

Lilavois paused, shaking her head at the terrible memory. "Ada was so upset. I had to hold her back. She begged them not to hurt him. RaZiel offered to trade his life for theirs, but they refused. They wanted Ada.

"Suddenly, her whole body began to glow. I couldn't hold on to her, Charmaine. She stretched out her hands and beams of light streamed through them. It hit the demons holding Simon and Matthias and killed them without her even touching them! We were at the opposite end of the square."

"My God!"

"I don't think she even knew what she was doing. I think her power and her desire to save Simon fused somehow and acted on its own. She fainted as soon as they were free."

Charmaine took a moment to sip her own tea, processing the implications of what Ada had been through before she looked back at Lilavois with a frown.

"Simon is the boy she fancies, the one who was with her in Kemet, right?"

"Yes," Lilavois replied with a smile. "They've been best friends since they were small children."

"Do you think it was coincidence that they took him and his father as hostages out of all the people here?"

"No. We didn't even know Simon was here. They recognized him from RaHabel."

"Of course," Charmaine nodded. "Simon must have heard the rumors and come here to find you."

"What rumors? How did you find us?" Lilavois asked.

"I would have left as soon as I got your telegram, but it took time to pull our war chest together. I had the weapons ready, of course, manufactured to your exact specifications, but I'd always assumed they'd be sent by boat. From the urgency in your message, I sensed we didn't have time for a lengthy journey. So, I sent a telegram to Captain Claybourne. Although he was halfway around the world, he agreed to meet me in Kemet. At the same time, I received a letter from Jhonna looking for you. She said she had not heard from Sabine and was hoping you could help find her. Naturally, I saw an opportunity to broaden our list of allies.

"There are more weapons than we could possibly wield on our own. I thought with Obi's demon army wreaking havoc everywhere, the Sisterhood might be grateful for the use of our arsenal. I told her how you were cast out in Liren and asked for help in finding you. She commands a small but efficient unit of the E'gida in the Arborlands. Captain Claybourne and I picked them up and headed to Liren to retrace your steps."

Charmaine paused as her lips curled in disgust. "When we got there, I asked for assistance in finding you, but no one would help. They were all just sitting around like cowards, too afraid to do anything that might risk retribution from the demons, even at the cost of their own freedom. There were wanted posters of you, RaZiel, and Ada everywhere.

"Jhonna went to Lieutenant Fenton's office to pay her respects and overheard them saying that someone had reported seeing you just outside of Bonn. Their sheriff was planning to round up a posse to capture you and trade you to the demons. I suspect Simon and his father must have heard the same rumor and set out in hopes of warning you."

Lilavois hummed in agreement, shaking her head bitterly. "And to think, I had planned to leave some of our weapons for them. Speaking of weapons, how many did you bring?"

"About a fifth of our arsenal, several hundred weapons of different kinds. Despite the grandeur of Captain Claybourne's ship, with the E'gida aboard, that's all we could carry."

"You've been able to produce so many?"

Charmaine finished her tea and set the cup delicately on the matching saucer. "Little sister, when you set me to a task, you should know I will see it through."

"Thank you for all you've done. We wouldn't have survived without you."

Charmaine reached for Lilavois's hands. "I would do anything for you and Ada. You know that."

Tears hung in Lilavois's eyes as she leaned down to kiss her sister's hand and bring it to her cheek.

"I know," she whispered back. "And I never stop being grateful for it. You know I would do the same for you."

"You'd better," Charmaine joked as she extracted her hand from Lilavois's grasp to straighten the felt and satin hat on her head. "I barely had time to pack a wardrobe before coming out here. I'm getting by with only a tiny trunk of clothes. Things are so desperate I find myself having to *mix and match* my wardrobe!"

Charmaine shuddered in mock outrage. "I've sent word to my butler, Allister, to meet us here with the rest of my things."

Lilavois chuckled as she took in her sister's cream and red silk pinstripe shirt with balloon sleeves. The shirt was topped with pearl buttons unfastened enough to make Charmaine's generous décolletage more of a weapon than a fact. All this finery rested under a black velvet vest embroidered with Adinkra symbols in black satin thread. Her pants were made of a black leather soft enough to mold to her voluptuous curves and paired with a fashionable pair of oilskin boots with wedge heels. The shoes were so polished, Lilavois felt sure Charmaine had never worn them before. Her ensemble was topped off with a polished leather gun holster slung diagonally over her hips.

"You look positively ready for war," Lilavois teased.

"You jest, but I assure you, everything on me has a battle-worthy purpose."

"The hat?"

Charmaine winked. "Fashion, of course. If I'm going to be a target, I need to make sure everyone can see me."

Their exhausted laughter rippled through the cabin until Jhonna entered. For a moment, she shifted awkwardly between them before addressing Lilavois directly.

"My apologies for interrupting, but I need a word with you."

Lilavois stood and gave Jhonna a hug. "Of course. Thank you for coming to our aid today."

"You're very welcome. But really, it's your sister you should thank." Jhonna held up Ada's crossbow and an arrow still coursing with Ada's magic. "We found these on the battlefield among the dead, those who were once demons. One of the Covenant said you killed them. He said you discovered a new form of magic and used it to create these weapons."

"We did," Lilavois answered cautiously.

Jhonna's eyes shifted from Lilavois to Charmaine. "And you say you have more of these weapons."

Charmaine stared at Jhonna's austere but sturdy blue cloak and rugged boots. A hard, earnest truthfulness rolled off the woman from the moment they met. Still, Charmaine refused to give Jhonna any information that Lilavois had not already shared. She turned to Lilavois, signaling for her to speak for them.

"We do," Lilavois replied.

Jhonna's stoic demeanor dissolved into something

desperate and needy. Carefully, she placed the crossbow and arrow on the table where Charmaine was still seated.

"Come back with me to the convent in Arborland. Reverend Sister Kai is at Haven House. Regardless of what happened before, we need your help to win this war! You know I haven't always trusted the Covenant, but even I can acknowledge the truth. The Covenant is fighting on our behalf, but there aren't enough of us to truly aid them. With weapons like these and the advances you've made in mooncraft... My God! We could finally put an end to all of this. I'm sure the Reverend Sister would overlook anything in your past to gain your help now."

Lilavois stared at Jhonna, thinking about the daughter who was resting just a few feet away. Could she trust the Sisterhood with her most precious secret?

Sensing her hesitation, Jhonna pressed on. "And you could help me look for Sabine. I'm sure, with the Reverend Sister at Haven House, we can find out where she is."

This drew Lilavois from her thoughts. "You still haven't heard from her?"

"No. I know she's busy, but it's unlike her to not answer my correspondence. If you come with me, then we can both find out where she's been stationed. I know she'd love to see you."

"Do you really think the Reverend Sister would listen to me after how I left?"

Jhonna was incredulous. "Captain Claybourne said it was

your mooncraft that created the shield that makes the Cypher invisible. You make arrows that kill demons and turn them human. After I testify to what I've seen, she won't have a choice! The Sisterhood and the Covenant can't fight this war alone. The Fallen are too many, but together with your weapons, we can finally win."

"I can take you," Captain Claybourne offered. He'd returned to the Cypher with RaZiel and approached them just in time to gather the gist of their conversation.

Lilavois shook her head. "The ship will need to function as a hospital for a little while longer. There are too many injured who can't be moved."

Jhonna instinctively stepped back as RaZiel moved closer and took Lilavois's hand.

"I'll take you," he said softly.

Lilavois smiled and placed her hand on his cheek. "RaZiel, I can't imagine our negotiations going well if I bring a demon to Haven House."

Their eyes lit up as they shared the same thought.

It wouldn't be the first time.

"I don't care what anyone thinks," RaZiel said. "We will not be parted again. Ada can come—"

Lilavois lowered her voice. "No. Once she's recovered, she needs to stay here and help prepare the rest of the arsenal. That way when the Sisterhood is ready, we can give SeKet and the others the help they need."

RaZiel frowned. He understood why Lilavois was being

so careful with her words; she didn't fully trust the Sisterhood. Of all of them, Ada was the most vulnerable. Yet if they were going to be successful, they needed the power only she could provide.

Seeing the reluctant agreement in his eyes, Lilavois continued. "I'll only be gone a few days. Plus, you'll be busy taking care of all the arrangements. By the time I return, we'll be ready to go. Once the last of the patients are moved safely, I'll meet you in Kemet."

To everyone's surprise, RaZiel pulled Lilavois close and kissed her.

Jhonna gasped, part revolted, part fascinated, as Lilavois returned his kiss with equal passion, but neither she nor RaZiel cared.

Few truly understood the sacrifice they were making.

CHAPTER SIXTEEN

FAREWELL

Charmaine and Captain Claybourne slipped outside to give Lilavois and RaZiel a few moments of privacy, but Jhonna didn't have that luxury.

She coughed loudly, reminding the lovers that she was in fact still present. "Excuse me, but when should we leave?"

With a sigh, Lilavois pulled herself from RaZiel's embrace. "As soon as we're able. After I say goodbye to Ada, I'll meet you outside."

With a curt nod, Jhonna went to her quarters to gather her things.

The nearest train station that could take them to Arborland was in Bevel. Lilavois and Jhonna had less than two hours to make it to the evening train, after which they would take a wagon the rest of the way to Haven House. If all went well, the trip there and back would take less than a week.

RaZiel raced back to their camp to pack Lilavois a bag and find two mounts while she stayed to check in on Ada, Simon, and Matthias, and to make sure that the members of the E'gida who remained knew how to care for the injured.

To her surprise, as Lilavois approached the door to the room where Ada was resting, she heard Simon's voice raised in anger. Lilavois opened the door to find Simon and his father in a standoff, with Ada sitting on the bed with her head hung low.

"What's going on here? You should all be resting."

Matthias turned from his son to face her.

"Thank you for your care, Lilavois, but my son and I will be heading home."

Lilavois opened her mouth to respond, but Simon got there first.

"No, we will not. I'm staying here with Ada."

Matthias's warm brown cheeks turned a deep burgundy. "That is out of the question! Before your mother died, I promised her I'd keep you safe."

Simon scoffed. "You're not around enough to keep me safe."

If Matthias was hurt by Simon's comment, his anger masked it well. "If I had known we would be walking into a demon trap, we never would have come. I know Ada's been like a sister to you all these years, but your aunt is right. Being around her is too dangerous."

"Ada saved our lives!" Simon shouted. "We'd be dead without her. Did you even see her? She killed a demon. Two of them! Why do you think they want us to shun her? They want her vulnerable enough to kill. They know her power can destroy them. That's why we need to help."

"We wouldn't have needed saving if we hadn't come here in the first place. This isn't our fight!"

"This is the only fight!" Simon roared. "You can look away from the truth if you want to, but I'm not leaving her. I don't care what you say."

"You think you're old enough to defy me? I'm still your father!"

"I don't *think* anything. I've already told you what I'm going to do."

Matthias's hand clenched as he stepped closer to Simon. "How dare you!"

Ada sprang from the bed and placed herself between them.

"No, Mr. Abara, please stop. There's no need for this."

She turned to Simon, his eyes boring into hers so deeply she almost lost her courage. But as her fingers traced the cuts on his face, the bruises on his neck, his injuries, Ada steeled her resolve.

What if her powers hadn't been enough? She couldn't bear the thought or risk taking the chance again.

As if reading her thoughts, Simon shook his head. "I'm fine, Ada. It's nothing."

"Simon, your father and your aunt are right. It's not safe for you with me."

Simon jerked back as if she'd slapped him. The hurt, the love, the fear was all there on his face for her to see.

"You don't mean it."

She really didn't, but she needed to. She could never lie to him with her eyes. He knew her too well. So, she closed them, hoping her words would be enough to push him away—to keep him safe.

"You know I'm right," she said. "I don't know how much worse this is going to get."

"But you killed them. You did that without a dagger, a sword, or anything."

"And what if I wasn't there? What if I faint again at the wrong time? I don't know what's going to happen, and I can't have you around when it does."

Simon opened his mouth to respond but couldn't find the words.

"You're not ready for that, and neither am I."

Instead of hearing the trembling lie in her voice, her words evoked the memory of a child long ago, a little boy who desperately wanted to protect the prettiest girl he'd ever seen, a girl humiliated without her leg. He'd chased the bully around a corner and ended up on the ground with a busted lip. Shock and shame kept him on the ground, unable to face her until a shadow descended from nowhere.

At the time, Simon thought he was going to die, but instead the shadow picked him up and set him on his feet.

"You will need to be much stronger than this if you mean to stand beside her," the shadow said, and was gone.

Though he never saw its face, the words had haunted him.

He'd never told Ada, and he didn't know until RaHabel that on that day in the schoolyard was the first time he'd met her father. Simon had failed her then, and he'd been working every day since to not fail her again.

No matter what he wanted to say, despite his best efforts, no matter how much he needed her, the truth was Simon had always known that she never needed him.

She can't even look at me.

Simon closed his mouth, afraid to see the same shame that he felt himself reflected in her eyes and walked away.

Once he was gone, Ada found addressing Matthias was easy.

"Mr. Abara, I'm truly sorry for all the trouble I've brought to you and your family. Please escort Simon home. He's safer there than he is with me. I can't risk anyone else I care about being hurt."

Matthias nodded before hastily brushing past Lilavois and RaZiel, only too happy to leave them all behind.

Lilavois rushed forward, holding her daughter, who was

already trembling with sobs of grief. RaZiel placed Lilavois's bag on the floor and embraced them both. His spirit was broken anew because he knew why his daughter had made the choice he'd made so long ago—and understood what it meant for her to make it.

"Oh, sweetheart!" It was all Lilavois could say as the conflict roiled within her. She didn't want to leave Ada in such a state and yet she couldn't end this war and give her daughter the life she deserved if she didn't.

"It'll be alright. When I get back—"

Ada stepped out of her parents' embrace. "You're leaving! Why? Where are you going?"

"I'm going to convince the Sisterhood to join our cause. Your aunt got them here to save us. Because of what they've seen, we might be able to convince them to fight with the Covenant."

Ada used her sleeve to wipe the tears that were still falling from her face. "I want to go with you. I thought we were supposed to stay together."

Lilavois took Ada's face in her hands. She had said those words more times than she could count, but she couldn't admit that Haven House wasn't safe for Ada, not with so many other worries on her mind.

"We are always together. Even when we're apart, we're together. But right now, we each have to play our parts. I need you to stay here because you're the only one who can enchant every weapon aboard this ship. Your father and Aunt

Charmaine are going to stay with you and help this city recover from what the Fallen have done. Then we'll all meet back in Kemet. Okay?"

"Okay," Ada sniffled. "How long will you be gone?"

"A week at the most, but in the meantime, I've got a favor to ask." Lilavois smiled as she lifted the Lasso of El from her belt. "Can you enchant this for me?"

Despite her sadness, Ada's eyes went wide with awe. "You're going to let me use it?"

"Ah, no! You need a lot more practice before that happens. Maybe one of the E'gida can help you before I get return, but in the meantime, I just need you to enchant it for me without poking your eye out. You think you can handle that?"

"I've never spelled leather before, but I'll try my best," Ada said, taking the sacred lasso from her mother. "But what if you need it?"

Lilavois laughed a little, happy she was able to distract Ada from her sadness and lighten the mood.

"I'm headed to a convent full of E'gida. If I'm in need, I'm sure they'll have one."

CHAPTER SEVENTEEN

HAVEN HOUSE

Ada was calmer by the time she and Jhonna rode off to Bevel, but Lilavois still felt nervous about leaving her in such a state. She knew the devastation on Simon's face all too well. She'd been in his position.

They're so young, too young to have to bear such burdens, she thought.

As soon as they arrived at the train station, Jhonna sent a telegram to the headmistress at Haven House to alert her of their impending arrival and the need for an audience with the Reverend Sister Kai. Lilavois stepped on the train determined to see this through and ensure Ada's safety.

After years of living a relatively anonymous existence in Liren, walking through the train cars with Jhonna was a bit jarring. As they made their way to their seats, Jhonna in her traditional E'gida garb with the Lasso of El at her waist garnered a steady stream of attention, with some beaming with appreciation while others recoiled in fear.

They'd barely settled into their couchette when the conductor made her way to them.

"Good afternoon, Sister. It's an honor to have you with us."

"Thank you," Jhonna smiled, clearly used to this kind of deference.

"I don't mean to pry, but to be honest, your presence has made some of our passengers a bit nervous. Reports are spreading that the Fallen set fire to Bonn."

"It's true, but the Sisterhood and the Covenant drove them back," Jhonna replied.

"The Covenant?" The conductor's eyes widened with alarm. "Should we be expecting any trouble here?"

"I believe we'll be safe," Jhonna replied. "Feel free to pass on the sentiment to the other passengers if you think it will help."

The conductor pulled at the bill of her hat and nodded. "Thank you, Sister. I'm sure it will."

As the conductor closed the door to their compartment, Lilavois leaned in.

"Do you think that's wise? We have no idea where the demons are or if we'll make it to Arborland safely."

Jhonna met Lilavois's gaze with a shrewd smirk.

"RaZiel came for you the last time our train was attacked. I see no reason to think he wouldn't do it again?"

Lilavois sat back in her chair, stunned into silence. Though it felt like a lifetime ago, it was their first encounter with the Covenant, and RaZiel's was not a face easily forgotten.

"And to think, all this time I thought you left the Covenant for some boy. It was him all along, wasn't it?"

Lilavois didn't respond. She still wasn't sure how much she could trust Jhonna. Though they had been good friends, Lilavois and Sabine had always been closer.

When Lilavois didn't respond, Jhonna shook her head. "I think we're past keeping secrets, don't you? Your daughter is about sixteen years old, the same age she would be if you carried her when we were in school. I just can't figure out how the child is his."

Jhonna paused, no longer looking at Lilavois as if she was holding an in-depth conversation with herself.

"I wouldn't have believed it if I hadn't seen them together with my own eyes. The resemblance is undeniable—the way he looks at her."

Jhonna turned back to Lilavois as if suddenly remembering she was there.

"I've seen the wanted posters. Is that why they want her? Because she's the first of her kind?"

Lilavois stared back, a little proud and even more

terrified. On one hand, Jhonna had put the pieces together so succinctly, the facts of her life almost seemed obvious.

On the other hand, Lilavois wasn't sure exactly where Jhonna's true allegiance lay—with the truth or the Sisterhood.

Yet Lilavois needed her help. They needed each other. The Covenant were far too few to hold back the threat Obi and his followers posed on their own. The Sisterhood could never defeat the Fallen without Ada's magic. Whether they liked it or not, their survival depended on their cooperation. Lilavois decided she might as well start with Jhonna.

"It's more than that," Lilavois said softly. "Much more."

⊗ ⊗ ⊗

They arrived at Haven House just after sunset. While Jhonna went to find Headmistress Castille, Lilavois took a moment to take in the surroundings. Though Lilavois had never been to Haven House, she was struck by how similar it was to the convent in North Kesar. The same stark but sturdy architecture. The same wide, cavernous dining room. The same smelly latrines.

"We can leave our bags here," Jhonna said in a rush as she returned. "The Headmistress received my telegram. Apparently, the Reverend Sister is anxious to meet you."

"And Sabine?"

Jhonna shook her head. "No one has seen her. She and

the Reverend Sister arrived together a few weeks ago, but no one has seen her since. Maybe she was sent on another assignment. You can ask the Reverend Sister yourself when you speak with her. She's in the North Tower. This way."

As they made their way deeper into the convent, they passed several apprentices who were clearly in their first or second years of study. In their round cheeks and sharp eyes, Lilavois saw herself, who she had been before she'd wandered into the garden late one night and changed her life forever.

Though they'd been traveling all day, Lilavois and Jhonna climbed the long distance up the winding, narrow stairs as if they had no time to spare.

The sooner Lilavois was able to form an alliance, the sooner they could stop hiding in the shadows. The sooner they could mount an effective attack on the Fallen, the sooner her family would be safe.

She took only a moment to catch her breath and smooth her overcoat before knocking on the small door at the top of the stairs.

At first, she was met with silence and the sound of wind whipping through the cavernous landing.

"She must be as out of breath as we are, climbing all those steps," Jhonna joked.

Only then did Lilavois register how far they had climbed, how high the tower was, and how strange it was for an elderly woman to set up her quarters in such an isolated and hard to reach part of the convent.

But before she could ponder it further, a calm voice spoke from behind the closed door. "Sister Jhonna, return to the main building to recover yourself. I will take this meeting alone. Sister Lilavois, please come in. I've waited so long to meet you."

Jhonna shrugged then turned toward the stairs. "Good luck," she whispered as Lilavois turned the doorknob and entered.

CHAPTER EIGHTEEN

ADA'S ARROW

The room was larger than she expected but dark when Lilavois entered, illuminated only by the reflection of overcast light from the moon.

"What a pleasure it is to finally meet you. I've heard so much about you."

Adjusting to the light, Lilavois turned to the voice, which emanated from a shadow behind the small desk at the opposite end of the room.

"The honor is mine, Reverend Sister," she replied.

"You don't mind the dark, do you, dear? My eyes are not what they used to be. At night, they grow tired."

"Not at all," Lilavois smiled, willing the prickle of unease in her stomach to settle. "At the convent, I spent many nights wandering the grounds in the dark."

Reverend Sister Kai inhaled deeply. "Indeed. Won't you take a seat?"

"I can hardly see to find one, Reverend Sister, but I don't mind standing."

"Nonsense, dear. How rude of me."

Lilavois watched a match come to life then settle over a candle at the center of the desk.

Above the flame, an ancient woman emerged with deep lines that crisscrossed through high cheekbones, sharp eyes, and a wide grin pulled tight across a weathered face. She beckoned with a welcoming hand.

"Much better. Thank you, Reverend Sister."

But Lilavois did not take a seat. Instead, her eyes traveled the room, noting its rounded stone walls and sharp corners. Bookshelves cast in flickering shadows lined the space from floor to ceiling with so many books and scrolls there was barely an open space save a few marble statues.

Lilavois's footsteps followed the curve of the room.

"This is quite the collection," she said, moving toward the closest shelf. Her fingertips traced a tightly wrapped scroll.

"Yes," the Reverend Sister agreed. "Sacred texts from all around the world."

"Are they just for reference, or is there a common theme among them?"

"We are Sisters of the Light. Our calling is the mastery of mooncraft. In these walls is every reference of its discovery and use since the beginning."

Lilavois could not mask her surprise. "Since the arrival of the Fallen?"

"Yes."

"How did you find them all?"

"With patience, child. I find that if you're careful, and wait long enough, what you need will usually come to you."

"I have never been a patient person," Lilavois admitted.

The Reverend Sister's laugh was an unsettling rumble of phlegm. "That's because you're so young, my dear, so very young. At my age, I almost feel like I've been here since the beginning of time itself. But you have something new to share, I'm told. A new weapon that may help advance our cause."

Lilavois drew closer. "Not so much new as an alliance between the Covenant and the Sisterhood. As you know, attacks from the Fallen have risen dramatically. I believe if we band together, we can stop them."

"I've heard rumors of a new kind of mooncraft, one that can actually kill the demons that have plagued us for so long. The papers have suggested that with this new power, we can finally end our conflict. At least, that's what the telegram from Sister Jhonna implied."

Lilavois held the Reverend Sister's gaze as she took the seat in front of her desk. Slowly, she reached for the small pouch at her waist and pulled out a handkerchief wrapped around an arrowhead. As she placed it on the desk between them, Lilavois could see its golden shimmer, even through the cloth. The color, the warmth, reminded her of Ada.

"This is the power Jhonna spoke of. When it pierces a demon's skin, it turns them human, so that they can die."

Something strange and fearful flashed across the Reverend Sister's face, so quickly Lilavois almost thought it was a flicker of candlelight.

The Reverend Sister Kai reached for the arrow. As she leaned forward, the heavy sleeves of her robe shifted to reveal the thin forearm and fingers of her left arm and the severed forearm of her right.

Every member of the Sisterhood knew how the Reverend Sister had lost her right arm fighting off the demon that almost took her life. The story was etched in the mind of every first-year apprentice of the convent. Still, to see the shriveled stump up close was a startling reminder that this woman had suffered to bring the legacy of the Sisterhood forth.

"Careful, Reverend Sister. The tip is laced with obsidian poison."

"Why?"

"I found it helps to penetrate the skin."

"I see." When the Reverend Sister picked up the handkerchief with the arrow, her nostrils flared.

"And you discovered this magic? Fused it to metal?"

"Yes," Lilavois answered. It wasn't entirely false, but something in her needed more of a reason to reveal the truth.

"I've been perfecting the process over many years, which is why we think now is the time for our forces to align."

"And the members of the Covenant, RaZiel, and SeKet, are aware of its power?"

Lilavois frowned. *How would the Reverend Sister know their names?* she wondered, before remembering that the papers had made them known long ago. "They are."

"And they are willing to take the risk of death at your hands?"

"Only if they wish it," Lilavois answered, surprised by the Reverend Sister's interest in how demons might feel, given that the Sisterhood's entire purpose was to kill them without hesitation or mercy. "Some see this new power as a sign of God's mercy—a chance to be given a soul and return."

The Reverend Sister smiled. "And you made these yourself?"

"Yes."

"Have you taught others to use their mooncraft in this way?"

"More can be made," Lilavois answered carefully. "As you know, I've been estranged from the Sisterhood for some time, and I've had no contact since. I reconnected with Jhonna only recently, but I can share this gift with as many of the Sisterhood as you will allow."

The Reverend Sister Kai folded the handkerchief with the arrow carefully inside it and placed it back on the desk. "That won't be necessary, my dear."

Lilavois stared in confusion. "Excuse me?"

"I grow weary of the stench of your lies."

Lilavois held the woman's gaze defiantly as she traced the Akoben symbol into the wooden arm of the chair she was holding.

"I don't know what you're talking about."

The Reverend Sister tilted her head. "No? Do you take me for a fool?"

"I took you for someone who wanted to end this war and free our world from the demons."

The breeze from the open windows picked up, letting her know it had heard her silent call.

The Reverent Sister traced the outline of the arrow between them.

"When Sabine brought word of Saisho's death," the Reverend Sister said, "I didn't know what to think. Nothing like it had ever happened before. I wonder if you can even comprehend what it means for someone like me, someone who has seen everything, to say something has *never happened before.*

"At first, I feared someone outside the Sisterhood had discovered the secret to mooncraft that had eluded us for so long. I asked her to secure his remains so that I could examine them. Unfortunately, Obi got there first and caused a mess. Who knew all our careful efforts to incite a war through the Stone Killings would be so easily upended by a troublesome little girl with an extraordinary power?"

Will alone kept Lilavois from trembling. "You—you were the Stone Killer?"

"Well, Sabine did the job, but I made the sacrifice."

She held up what remained of her right arm.

"As her mother, I can understand your instinct to protect your child," the Reverend Sister said. "But imagine my surprise when I learned that it was one of our own, *my* own, a Sister of the Light, who betrayed us by consorting with a demon to create the one thing God has denied us in all our forsaken time here—the chance to create life."

Lilavois swallowed the bile creeping up from her stomach in a wave of revulsion. All this time, they'd used their power, dedicated their lives to serve the very enemy—the first enemy —they'd been sworn to destroy.

The façade masquerading as Reverend Sister Kai watched Lilavois with waning interest. "Nothing to say? I suppose not."

"Why?" Lilavois finally asked, trying to see past the illusion before her to the demon underneath. "Why would you have founded an order whose sole purpose is to kill your own kind?"

"Mooncraft, of course. I made a mistake. We made a mistake. Your kind makes mistakes all the time! Your entire existence is defined by a series of never-ending mistakes, and yet you're forgiven. You have endless chances to try again, in this life or the next. But us, we were damned for eternity.

Never to be forgiven. Never to be whole again. And then God gave you mooncraft!

"Of course, everyone blamed me. After my exile, I needed a new pursuit. We knew God had gifted mooncraft to the humans so they could protect themselves against us. But none of us could figure out how. I've always been more curious than most of my kin. Some might say that's how I got our kind into this mess in the first place. But I've never been inclined to take no for an answer.

"I decided if I couldn't have mooncraft, I could control it. I wanted to know its full potential. But humans are so undisciplined—yet so desperate to find a way to take a stand against us. Creating a school where I could dedicate humans to the mastery of mooncraft was a perfect way to take back what was denied me."

"You had us fighting your own kind? Why would you do that?"

In truth, Lilavois didn't care about the answer. She just needed to keep the Reverend Sister talking until she could figure out a way to drive Ada's arrow through her treacherous chest.

The Reverend Sister shrugged. "They cast me out. It was a small price to pay. It's not like I ever killed any of my own. Even RaZiel can't say that."

Lilavois held her breath, realizing how completely she had been lured here.

"Come now. You can't be so surprised that I know. His smell is all over you."

Refusing to even acknowledge her beloved in this demon's presence, Lilavois shook her head and tried to refocus the conversation.

"Who are you?"

"Think, my proud apprentice, my learned E'gida. Who else but the Lightbringer would form the Sisters of the Light?"

Her body shuddered in terror as the name, the answer that had been in front of them from the very beginning flooded her mind.

Lucifer.

How could they all have been so led astray?

CHAPTER NINETEEN

THE DEVIL YOU KNOW

Lilavois's mind struggled to refocus, to push past the shock of coming face to face with the very demon who led the Fallen from the Ever. The same demon who formed the Sisterhood she'd sworn her allegiance to so long ago.

Her eyes filled with tears of pain, of rage, of grief, but she shook them away because, as sharp as the feeling of betrayal was, it would not save her.

"Why the Stone Killer killings?" she asked, stalling for time to formulate a plan. "What purpose did they serve?"

Lucifer frowned as if the answer was obvious. "Recruitment, of course. Every time the world thinks there is a rise in demon attacks, we get new recruits—and I get a chance to expand my knowledge. Our apprentices are so dedicated to the fight. Just like you, until you slipped through my fingers. I'd hoped you would bring RaZiel and your daughter to me so I could end this once and for all. Imagine my disappointment when I was informed you traveled alone. I feared Sabine might have been successful in warning you about me, but that at least did not prove to be a hindrance."

He glanced down at the arrow between them. "But now I see your daughter is much more of a problem than Obi realized."

Again, Lilavois shifted the conversation away from her family. "Where is Sabine?"

"She's just there," Lucifer cooed, pointing to a stone statue hidden in the shadows at the corner of the room. "I would have disposed of her weeks ago, but I thought you might like to say goodbye. I know you didn't part on the best of terms when you were at the convent together, but you should know that Sabine always spoke of you fondly."

Lilavois leapt from the chair toward the statue. Though her face was marble, the features were undeniably the same as the dear friend she once knew.

"Damn you!" Lilavois cursed as she whipped around, reaching for her lasso, only to realize with a sudden panic that it wasn't there. With her left hand bare and trembling, she used her right to grab the demon claw dagger from her pocket and hold it out.

Lucifer rose slowly. "I already am," he hissed.

Lilavois backed away, trying to put more distance

between them, but her intent was not to escape. He knew too much about Ada. She could not let him leave this room.

"Why are you doing this?" she asked. "You should be happy that God has shown you mercy and given you a chance to return to the Ever."

As Lucifer stepped closer, the visage of the Reverend Sister Kai fell away, revealing a creature of smoke with piercing yellow eyes and long claws gleaming within his shadows.

"Because in this realm, there is no mercy that I do not grant," he said.

Lilavois murmured the spell that activated the symbol she'd traced on the wood of her seat. Her summoning was most powerful when it was grounded to the earth, but her connection to the elements was strong. Even from so high up, it sent a gust of wind through the room, assuring her that the call of her magic had been heard. Now she needed it to gather and grow. Because she would need power, much more than she'd ever summoned before, if she was going to survive this encounter.

"You ungrateful cur!" Lucifer snarled. "How dare you use the mooncraft that *I* taught you against me?"

"You didn't teach me anything! You betrayed the women who taught me! Sister Ignatia, Sister Carpethianna, all of them!"

Lilavois's eyes darted around, searching for another weapon she could use, until they settled on the Lasso of El that still hung from the belt around Sabine's frozen body. Pretending to stumble back between the bookshelf and Sabine's body, Lilavois grabbed the lasso quickly, holding it behind her back as she felt the pulse of mooncraft still present within its fibers. With a sigh of relief, she let the leather uncoil.

A mirthless laugh echoed through the shadow and smoke bellowing out in front of her. "I remember Sister Ignatia. Troublesome woman. I don't know when she began to suspect me, but it was no matter. She died—defending you, I believe—before anything could come of it. I suppose I should thank you."

Lilavois's mind strained to recall the last conversation she had with Sister Ignatia just before she passed away. Something about a question she was investigating, something that would be revealed. At the time, Lilavois was too filled with grief to delve deeper. When had Sabine discovered the secret? Lilavois's gaze flickered to Sabine's body, her friend's arms frozen in her last defense, and mourned that she would never know.

"This is *our* legacy!" Lilavois roared. Stepping forward, she raised Sabine's lasso to strike. "Using it for your own gain doesn't make it yours."

Lilavois and Lucifer lunged at the same moment, but Lilavois's lasso crossed the distance first, burning through the smoke of Lucifer's demon form to the flesh beneath. He growled, stumbling back and to the left.

Perfect, Lilavois thought. She needed to get him closer to the door, the farthest point from the desk and Ada's arrow. She lashed out with her lasso again and again in a relentless barrage that made her arms ache. Furious, Lucifer's claws slashed through the air trying to capture it, but each time the slim tail of her whip slipped through his fingers. Slowly, her advance shifted their respective positions like hands moving backward on a clock, until finally Lilavois was within arm's reach of Ada's arrow.

Realizing her plan and his mistake, Lucifer rose into the air above her, his face coalescing from the smoke into a mask of charred bone.

"You will not defeat me," he sneered before dissolving into a cloud of smoke and rushing forward.

The movement was so fast Lilavois barely saw the shift, but by then the summoning of her mooncraft had gathered enough force. She could feel its power waiting to be unleashed just outside the tower window. All she needed to do was utter the word to release it.

Lucifer appeared again before her, claws extended and close enough she could feel the heat of his hatred burn against her skin.

"Akoben," Lilavois whispered, then dove toward the side to avoid being driven into him by the force of what was to come. The wind rushed in through the windows with the full force of a gale, thrusting Lucifer back and pinning him to the wall. Keeping low, Lilavois used her momentum to reach across and grab the glowing metal that rested on Lucifer's desk.

This was her one chance to either run from the room or kill the devil himself. Yet knowing he would come after her family, and that she had unwittingly revealed the extent of Ada's power to the one person who could unleash both the Sisterhood and the Fallen to hunt her, it was hardly a choice. Lilavois stepped into the torrent. With the wind at her back, she leapt, bringing the arrow down toward the shadow of his leg with all her might.

Before Lucifer could feel the bite of Ada's arrow, a tendril of his smoke lashed out, hitting Lilavois across the chest with such force she was knocked into the stone bookcases behind her.

The right side of her body took the brunt of the blow, lacerating skin, shattering bone, and puncturing organs. Seized with pain, her vision blurred as she felt the lasso and arrow slip from her hands. With nothing to brace her, Lilavois crashed to the ground, and as she fell, the winds withered with her.

The room felt suddenly quiet. Sounds were muffled, but she couldn't process the fact that her senses were fading. Instead, her awareness narrowed to the fact that her hands were empty and she had little time. The effort to move was immense, but she forced herself to lift her head, searching for the ember of light the arrow held as it glowed in the darkness. Lilavois found it just above her head, grasped it quickly and turned onto the side of her body that hurt less.

She was not quick enough.

Lilavois screamed in pain as Lucifer landed on top of her chest before she could right her body, before she could even lift her hand to strike. In the dark, his claws shimmered above her.

The taste of blood was sharp in her mouth, but Lilavois did not care. Ada's arrow burned in her palm like a star. She lifted her hand. If this was her last breath, she would use it to fight for her family.

"They said you were stubborn."

Though she could barely make out the sickening yellow of his eyes, Lilavois could hear the satisfaction in his voice clearly. It worked on her nerves like a serpent's fangs sinking paralyzing venom into her veins.

"I suppose you wouldn't be one of my own if you didn't try your best." His claws twitched in anticipation. "But I have a feeling my best will be better."

Then, in a flash, he was gone.

CHAPTER TWENTY

ALWAYS

Lilavois blinked.

Above her, where Lucifer had once been, there was nothing but darkness. The respite from pain was startling. Yet below the receding calm, the air trembled with violence. If she tried hard, she could hear an undercurrent of growing chaos. She tried to listen, tried to hear, but trying anything was becoming harder and harder to do.

Something was happening, but she couldn't hold onto it. Her body was growing numb, the ancient pattern of death unfolding. It had done all it could do, and now, in her last moments, it gave Lilavois peace. Peace enough to close her eyes and cry.

She had not killed Lucifer, and, in her failure, he'd gotten away.

How would she protect Ada?

Her sobs struggled against her lack of air until a quiet thought pierced her grief.

Why? Why would Lucifer flee a dying woman?

Lilavois opened her eyes.

He wouldn't.

The sharp taste of adrenaline mixed with the blood in her mouth as her senses reignited. To her right, she heard the flapping of large wings. She felt the floor beneath her shudder as something massive collided with the tower. Lilavois turned her head toward the window. Outside, two birds larger than anything that evolved on Earth were locked in a fierce battle, claws out and beaks snapping. Though she didn't recognize the one with pale gray feathers, she knew the bird with black-brown feathers by heart.

But above all else, she heard the sudden sound of Ada calling her name.

"Mama!" Ada's face came into view as she knelt beside Lilavois.

Lilavois sensed she was dying, but she hadn't truly grasped the finality of the moment until she saw the look on her daughter's face. Shock turned quickly to horror and then anguish as Ada's face collapsed into tears.

"No!" Ada moaned, burying her face in her mother's hair. "No! Please, no!"

Lilavois raised her arm to soothe her daughter. "Listen—"

A bloodstained cough erupted in her throat. She tried to

roll to her left, but the pain was too great. Carefully, Ada slid her hand under Lilavois's back and lifted her enough to expel some of the blood pooling in her mouth.

"Don't talk. It's okay," Ada whispered, her voice quivering.

Lilavois tested her breath. It was shallow, but steady enough to hold her voice. "Lucifer," she rasped.

"We know. That's why we came. Your classmate, Sabine, sent a letter to Aunt Charmaine. She found it in the things delivered to her three days after you left Bonn. Sabine knew," Ada sobbed. "She tried to warn you, but we got her letter too late."

Lilavois smelled the faint scent of roses just before her sister came into view. Charmaine knelt on the opposite side of Ada and held Lilavois's hand with silent tears trailing down her face.

"Charmaine..." Lilavois continued looking between her and Ada with frantic eyes as she tried to hold on to lucidity. "I tried to kill him. He...he knows about Ada. You have to find him. He got away!" Lilavois wanted to say more, but another rush of blood pooled in her mouth. The effort to cough was prolonged and more painful with each gasp for air.

"No, he didn't," Charmaine whispered, mopping the blood from her sister's cheek with a lavender-scented handkerchief. "RaZiel has him now. Rest, little sister. No one will hurt our girl. Ever."

That's right, Lilavois thought, vaguely recalling a flutter of beautiful sable and black wings. With a sigh, she closed her eyes.

"Mama!" Ada pleaded. "Stay with me, please. They've called for the doctor. Don't leave us."

Weak eyes found her daughter's face in the darkness. Of all the pain they'd faced together, this was the first pain, the only pain, Lilavois could do nothing about. "I have always been and will always be with you," she said softly. "Even when you can't see me. I will be with you."

It was her final message, the only thing worth saying, as her eyes closed, and all sensation slowly slipped away.

CHAPTER TWENTY-ONE

AFTER

Ada knew the exact moment her mother died. From the slackening of Lilavois's body in her arms to the crack in her own heart to the anguished sob Aunt Charmaine released as she collapsed over her sister. But more than anything else, she heard it in the piercing sound of her father's agony screeching across the sky the moment her mother's heart stopped beating.

After, there was no sound at all. No furious caws. No beating wings, no tearing of beaks and claws.

Because Lucifer had taken everything from them.

Only an hour ago, it seemed as if they might arrive in time. RaZiel flew ahead of the Cypher to reach Lilavois first, to save her. They had hoped. Well before the airship landed, Ada watched her father through the ship's telescope as he raced into the tower window. When he came out a second later, he carried in his beak the shadow of a man, a demon with yellow eyes. RaZiel had dropped him from the sky, only to have Lucifer transform into a bird mid-air. Whether Lucifer's intention was to fight or fly away, Ada did not care. She knew her father would deal with him. If RaZiel didn't have Lilavois, that meant she was still somewhere inside. Ada left RaZiel and Lucifer hurtling through the sky as the Cypher landed outside Haven House's gates. She'd bounded from the airship and raced through the convent, trying to find her mother.

But now, in the silence, there was nothing more any of them could do, which meant one of two things. Either RaZiel was dead too or he had stopped fighting.

Ada released her mother into Charmaine's embrace before running to the window. She couldn't lose them both. She couldn't.

She saw RaZiel in his human form, spiraling from the sky in a free fall as Lucifer chased him from above, talons extended and closing in.

If Lucifer was still chasing him, then her father was not dead. Something feral and desperate burst open inside Ada. She knew this feeling. She'd felt it before in Bonn when she thought Simon would die.

"Don't you touch him!" she screamed in a voice she barely recognized. Ada reached for the crossbow she usually kept strapped to her back only to find it missing. A flash of panic stabbed through her before she remembered she didn't need it. She extended her hand and called her power forth, piercing Lucifer through his ribs with a single beam of light just as his talons began to close around RaZiel's chest.

Lucifer shrieked in pain as his transformation began, but that was none of Ada's concern. Lucifer, the demon who had killed her mother, would be dead soon. Instead, she kept her eyes on RaZiel, who was still plummeting through the air like a stone.

"Papa!" Ada screamed.

At first, she wasn't sure he'd heard her, but then she saw it —the subtle shift in his body as he reached out to her. His eyes met hers as his arms burst into feathers and his dead gaze hardened into something of purpose. Ada stepped back as he flew through the tower window. RaZiel landed in front of her before transforming into himself again.

Immediately, he pulled Ada into his arms and held her there as she let out all the tears he could not. In her eyes he saw the same grief, the same loss that he felt—only brand new and etched within a face that was too young for the pain it bore. He knew what it meant to lose the one thing you loved more than anything—more than your own life. He'd done it twice now.

Only one thing—the most important thing—made this time completely different.

It had taken his daughter's voice calling him back to remember that he could not just disappear. There was not just one but two heartbeats that he lived for, and while one was gone, the other, though hurt and maybe even broken, was still very much alive. The tightness of Ada's arms as she clung to him filled RaZiel with the stark realization that she needed him, and if he were to survive an eternity without Lilavois, he would need her, too.

Over the top of Ada's head, RaZiel's eyes fixed on the place where Lilavois lay, partially hidden by Charmaine's sobbing form. As his awareness fanned out from the tight circle of Ada, Charmaine, and Lilavois, RaZiel saw Jhonna guarding the doorway with three other E'gida. From the press of bodies that crowded the hall and tiny stairwell, it seemed that Jhonna had brought half the convent with her. Those who could see into the room stared in shock between Lilavois's dead body and the demon hugging a girl with an undeniable likeness to him.

RaZiel met the open hostility of their gazes with a defiant protectiveness. What they thought of him did not matter. It was only Ada he feared for and Charmaine he sought to protect now. This was the family Lilavois had left him, and he would not fail again to defend them.

One of the E'gida leaned in and whispered in Jhonna's ear. "Are you sure it wasn't him who killed her?"

Though her voice was low, RaZiel could hear her clearly.

Jhonna looked at Lilavois's body, peaceful in her final repose, Ada's arrow still clutched in her hand. "He's not capable of it," she replied.

Charmaine looked up with red, swollen eyes. "This was Lucifer's work," she added, her voice cold with rage. "The very person who founded the Sisterhood, who you all followed blindly, was using the gift of mooncraft against us!"

The impact of her words rippled through the room and into the hall. Murmurs of confusion, shock, and anger filtered back.

A young woman who stood beside Jhonna stepped forward. "You dare sully the memory of the Reverend Sister Kai in the presence of this demon?"

Charmaine sprang to her feet in an instant and stepped toe to toe with the E'gida, tears still wet on her angry face.

"I do dare. Often." Her voice was ragged, but lethal. "Your beloved Reverend Sister Kai was Lucifer himself! He killed my sister. She didn't know when she entered this room what she was up against, but she was smart enough to discover the truth on her own in one night. What's your excuse? You've probably been here bowing down to him your entire life."

The E'gida before her shook with indignation as Jhonna stepped in between them.

"Charmaine, please!" Jhonna pleaded. "She doesn't know."

"Then tell her. My sister is dead. I've no patience for stupidity."

"You come here under our hospitality and bring a demon—"

"Stand down, Neveah," Jhonna interrupted. "All is not as it seems. This man is no ordinary demon. He is RaZiel of the Covenant."

"Are you mad?" Neveah snapped. "You saw the Reverend Sister's body broken in the field outside our gate." Neveah pointed to RaZiel. "He killed her!"

Jhonna sighed. Her shoulder and neck ached with the tension of holding so many lies at bay so the truth might finally come through. Beside her, the two other E'gida who had rushed to the convent gates when the Cypher arrived and had seen Lucifer transform before their eyes shifted uncomfortably.

Jhonna placed a calming hand on each of Neveah's shoulders but spoke loud enough for those gathered in the hall and stairwell to hear. "Listen to me. Some of you may have seen Reverend Sister Kai's body, yes, but most of you didn't see her fall. You did not see her *transform*. The human body you saw was not her true form. She was the demon, Lucifer, right under our noses the entire time."

Neveah jerked back. "Blasphemer! The demon has you under his spell." She looked to the other two E'gida for confirmation but found only pity. "Then how is she dead? How is she human?"

Jhonna looked over to where Ada stared back at her from within the safety of her father's arms. This was the worst time to have this discussion, to expect so much from a girl who had just lost her mother, and yet, they had no more time to waste.

At Jhonna's silent plea, Ada stepped out of RaZiel's embrace.

Jhonna turned back to Neveah. "That is what we've come to show you. It's time to fulfill our mission once and for all."

CHAPTER TWENTY-TWO

THE RECKONING

Before Ada could walk away, RaZiel grabbed her hand. "Are you sure?"

The warmth, the love, in his eyes threatened to bring her own grief back to the surface, but she couldn't afford that. Not now.

"Whether I am or not, it can't matter," Ada replied.

"It does to me. No one else but us knows what we've lost."

She stared back at him with a sober resolve. "But we're not the only ones who have suffered. If everything in Sabine's letter is true, if everything we believe Obi is capable of is true, we have to stop this so no one else has to feel what we feel."

"I'll go with you—"

"Having a demon with us will only make this talk more difficult. It will go better if Aunt Charmaine and I go alone."

"I will not let you out of my sight," RaZiel replied, looking around the room. "Your mother wasn't sure the Sisterhood could be trusted."

"I know, but she trusted her," Ada said, turning to Jhonna. "By the way you're staring at me, I know my mother told you the truth about me?"

"She did," Jhonna replied.

"And have you told anyone else here?"

"Lilavois wanted to see if the Reverend Sister Kai could be trusted first. I promised her I would say nothing until she decided." Jhonna's voice caught as she looked at Lilavois's body. "We were very close once. Though at the time I didn't understand her reasons for leaving the convent, I would never risk something she gave everything to protect."

Ada watched Jhonna for a moment before nodding, ignoring the stares she felt from the other members of the Sisterhood.

"I can tell by the way everyone except you and my family are looking at me."

Scanning the room, RaZiel detected no lie in Jhonna's words, but more than that, he saw the utter confusion on the faces of the other members of the Sisterhood.

So ignorant, he thought. *So vulnerable.*

Ada reached up to kiss his cheek before taking her aunt's hand. "Look after Mama," she whispered. "We'll be back as soon as we're able."

Jhonna led the E'gida and the other members of the convent out first, leaving Charmaine and Ada to follow. They lingered only long enough to see the first of RaZiel's tears fall as he lifted Lilavois's body from the floor and cradled it tenderly in his arms.

⚙ ⚙ ⚙

They assembled in the dining hall, with every occupant of Haven House present. After the Sisterhood brought Lucifer's body into the room, Jhonna read Sabine's letter aloud.

The revelation from one of their own was devastating, but even this news was overshadowed when Ada stepped forward to reveal who she was.

Jhonna and a few of the E'gida who had fought in Bonn gave their first-hand accounts of the weapons they discovered and how they had killed the demons around them. Most importantly, they described seeing the Reverend Sister transform from a bird into a demon into a human after Ada used her power to kill him.

Naturally, members of the convent had many questions. But as Ada, Jhonna, and Charmaine took the time required to answer them, they found most of the Sisterhood not as reticent as they feared.

In the three days it took for Jhonna and Lilavois to travel to the convent, a surprising development had taken hold. Accounts of the demons' defeat in Bonn had spread. While the stories of the heroics varied, there was a common thread that bound each tall tale together, a weapon that could kill a demon had finally been found.

Speculation about the news was rampant, with some claiming the Sisters of the Light used mooncraft to develop a new technology. Others said the Covenant had discovered their own form of magic. Regardless of which story was told, they all had one thing in common. Almost every town, village, and governing body demanded access to this weapon for themselves.

Almost.

In contrast to those who wanted the demon scourge to end, there were others, like the residents of Liren, who insisted the Covenant was a threat to their safety. To secure their own advantage, they advocated partnership with the Fallen against the Covenant and anyone else who challenged demon supremacy. Members of Haven House had watched the discourse with growing concern. Charmaine tried her best to quiet their fears.

"This is a delicate time," she began. "But the papers don't tell the full story. Even within these smaller alliances, Obi, the leader of the Fallen, is losing ground."

"How do you know this?" Neveah asked.

"Because the same stories you've read have reached the demon world as well. Those same stories brought the Fallen to us in Bonn. When they arrived, they found one of their kin and a member of the Covenant, Kibuka, working with the E'gida to help the community in Bonn recover from the destruction. They came seeking the mercy of redemption that the Covenant spoke of in RaHabel."

A murmur ran through the gathering.

"You've been to RaHabel?" Neveah asked.

"No, but Ada has. She went there to rescue her parents after the Fallen captured them for murdering one of their own."

Neveah scoffed. "Every first-year apprentice knows that the Fallen don't kill their own kind. The demons say it is forbidden. Even in the fighting now, there are no reports of the Covenant killing members of the Fallen."

"It's true," Ada replied. "When I was little, they came to our home. Tried to kill me with demon poison. My father, RaZiel, killed three of his own to save me."

Neveah frowned. "What do you mean 'tried' to kill you? Demon poison is lethal. No human can survive it."

Ada paused, remembering a time when she was afraid of what it meant for RaZiel to be her father. "You forget that I'm half-demon. The poison did affect me. I lost my leg because of it, but I survived. In RaHabel, I told them who I was. Another member of the Covenant, SeKet, tried to convince them that my power could be a way for them to return to the Ever. Some believed us, most did not, but after what happened in Bonn, their disbelief is beginning to change.

"At first, they just wanted to see if the rumors were true. We showed them the weapons I spelled so that anyone who uses them can do what I can. Eventually, a few wanted to experience the transformation for themselves. Kibuka and I granted their wish. Those who witnessed it promised to share what they saw with others."

Charmaine put her arm around her niece, so proud of Ada's courage. "The tide of the Fallen is beginning to turn. What Ada can do, the power she's able to share with all of us, has never happened before. Now, more and more of the Fallen want the hope Ada offers. If we work together, we can offer them a chance they've never had and finally rid the world of demons."

For Neveah, the chance was almost too good to be real, but it was a chance she couldn't refuse. She raised her hand to ask the only question left.

"How do we get started?"

CHAPTER TWENTY-THREE

BURNING

Jhonna spent the rest of the day and the evening coordinating with the Sisterhood at Haven House to send telegrams to the other convents, strategize the quickest way to mobilize the E'gida, and commission three airships to transport them to the front lines where the Covenant members were still fighting. Their goal was to have their plans finalized by the time the airships arrived the following morning. While Jhonna and the other E'gida finalized their strategy, Headmistress Castille showed Ada their full arsenal of weapons.

"If there's any assistance you require, please let us know. I can assign you an apprentice if you'd like." Though the headmistress's stare was intense, it was not unkind.

"Thank you," Ada said quietly. "I just need time."

The headmistress closed the door behind her and left Ada alone.

Though hers was the most strenuous task among the group, she welcomed it. As she worked her craft over the swords and daggers, lassos and arrows of Haven House, she could almost imagine that her mother was there watching her. When she closed her eyes, Ada heard Lilavois's voice guiding her.

"That's it," her mother would have said. "Feel the grain beneath your fingers. Let your magic run through you until you coat every fiber, every thread of metal."

"How will I know I'm done, Mama?" she asked, mimicking their conversation from what felt like a lifetime away.

"You'll know when the magic pushes back against you, like a cup that's already filled and can't take any more."

The first time Ada felt the sensation, she was in the forest outside Bonn with a metal arrow in her hand. It took practice for her to learn the techniques required to work her magic through different surfaces. Each material from metal to fabric to wood required a distinct approach, like learning to sing the same song in different keys. It took even longer to hone her knowledge of the more subtle differences needed to bind her magic with mahogany versus pine or copper versus iron or the living material of leather.

But Lilavois had been an excellent teacher. Between her gentle encouragement, the notes and references in her grimoire, and their schedule of consistent practice, Ada was well prepared for the task. Moving between each crate of weapons, she used her power with the confident ease her mother taught her. When she finished the last box, the room was bathed in a saffron glow from the power each weapon carried.

Looking at all she had done, all her mother had taught her, Ada burst into tears of gratitude for the legacy her mother left her and grief that her mother was no longer here to see it fully realized.

With no time to waste and even less time to mourn, Charmaine left Ada to work on Haven House's arsenal while she did the one thing they could not leave undone.

She returned to the tower to find RaZiel sitting on the ground with Lilavois still cradled in his arms. Though he did not look up when she entered, Charmaine knew he was still crying. She heard his grief echoing off the tower walls as she climbed.

Before Bonn, she'd never met RaZiel, this demon who changed the trajectory of her sister's life. The first time she saw RaZiel, Charmaine was looking down on him from aboard the Cypher. He was kissing Lilavois. They were surrounded by demons in the most impossible situation imaginable, and he was kissing her. Charmaine had always hoped RaZiel was worth the many risks Lilavois had taken to be with him, but in that moment, at first sight, Charmaine knew he was. If she had any doubts, she might not have been able to bear the task of sharing this sacred last rite with him—preparing to bury her only sibling, and her best friend.

She knelt in front of RaZiel and placed her hand gently on the part of Lilavois's head that she could reach, the part that was not tucked under RaZiel's chin in an all-encompassing embrace.

"It's time," she whispered through her own fresh tears.

RaZiel looked up then, staring back at her with eyes that should have been red. Instead, they were clear-white, warm-brown, and perfect, with traces of a faintly luminous liquid streaming down his face.

At once, she saw the angel Lilavois had told her about, the man who glowed from within.

When he made no move to release Lilavois's body, Charmaine thought for a second that perhaps he had not heard her, but his open stare and his lack of response told her something else.

He heard her, yet he did not understand.

Do the Fallen ever bury their own? she wondered before remembering the piles of dust of his kin in Bonn. *No,* she realized. Until Ada, their deaths left nothing in its wake, nothing to mourn, nothing but memory and time.

"We have to bury her."

RaZiel's face crumbled as he turned away, clutching Lilavois's body closer.

"Her body still has warmth."

"I want her back as much as you do, but she's gone. We have to say goodbye."

"But it isn't goodbye. Not for you. You will see her again. Not as this, but more. As the beautiful soul she truly is."

Charmaine smiled despite the ache of longing in her chest. "I hope you're right."

RaZiel met her gaze. "I am."

His words stilled her as a new understanding of the man —no, the being—before her emerged. Though it would be many years from now, God willing, she would be reunited with her sister, her family, and everyone she'd ever loved, but RaZiel never would. When she was gone, when Ada was gone, he would linger here alone. Unless... Would he use one of Ada's weapons to free himself? It seemed impossible that this had not occurred to him, but perhaps he was in too much distress.

"With Ada's power, you will see her again too. One day."

"You don't know that," he said softly. "No one but Abba knows. There was never a place for redeemed souls in the Ever. Before our rebellion, there was never a need. Even with Ada's power, I don't know where we will be. I don't know if Lilavois will be there."

Charmaine looked at him anew, seeing him truly for the first time since Lilavois's death—the trembling of his body, the way his whole being seemed to shape itself around Lilavois' form. It had been hours and he was still in the same position, frozen in his grief.

Death was a part of life. Human life. But he was something else entirely.

"I'm sorry," she whispered. "But we have to bury her properly before we leave here. You have to let go."

"I've tried," he rasped, his eyes desperate and wild. "I can't... I can't make my arm release her."

Charmaine leaned in, caressing Lilavois's head and the part of her sister's hand that she could reach.

"I know you love her. We all do," she said softly. "Let me show you how."

⚙ ⚙ ⚙

While Ada finished working on Haven House Convent's arsenal, Charmaine led RaZiel down to the clinic, where they prepared Lilavois for burial. After washing her clean, they anointed her body with herbs and essential oils then dressed Lilavois in a simple white gown, as was customary in the Isle of Moor, before placing a crown of lavender and ivy on her head.

When Ada was done, she and Charmaine bathed as well, donning two white gowns they borrowed from the Sisterhood. Then they led the burial procession of mourners to the convent gardens. Captain Claybourne choked out a few words to honor Lilavois's skill as an apothecary and surgeon and her character as a friend. Jhonna followed, speaking on behalf of the Sisterhood and Lilavois's family, who were too heartbroken to do much more than withstand the ceremony. RaZiel carried Lilavois in his arms throughout the procession, until it was time to place her down on the wood pyre, stacked high and tight to ensure the moonfire would be hot enough to consume her fully.

Once the last rituals were said and the fires lit, Charmaine and Ada sat closely together, comforting each other in their grief. No one expected RaZiel to climb into the pyre, to hold Lilavois as she burned, but as Ada watched him through the flicker of flames and the steady downpour of her own tears, she realized she should have because she was burning too, with shock, with anger, and with sadness for all this war had taken from them.

Lilavois's body crumpled to ash just as the sky gave up the last of its darkness. RaZiel emerged from the dying embers naked and seemingly unharmed. Only Ada truly understood how much of him had burned away in the fire.

CHAPTER TWENTY-FOUR

A SONG FOR ANGELS

Lilavois had done her part. She'd given her life to save her family and the Sisterhood from Lucifer himself. As they walked away from the burial, each of the mourners knew it was now time to do theirs. The first of the commissioned airships arrived with the sun as everyone prepared to go their separate ways.

Jhonna, Kibuka, and all available E'gida within the convent took their newly enchanted weapons and headed to the front lines in Bel Mar, where the fighting with the Fallen was reported to be the most intense.

Captain Claybourne and the Cypher's crew were set to take RaZiel and Ada back to Charmaine's warehouse in Kemet, where Ada would enchant the full store of weapons Lilavois designed. From there, the Cypher would ferry most of their party to Bel Mar to join the others. If their plan worked, more members of the Fallen and the Sisterhood, and perhaps even some civilians, would join their cause. Charmaine would stay in Kemet to continue production and oversee weapons shipments to wherever they were needed.

As they boarded the Cypher, the weariness of the ordeal they'd been through weighed on RaZiel, Charmaine, and Ada like an iron blanket. Since leaving Bonn, Charmaine and Ada had not slept for forty-eight hours. They accepted the quarters that Captain Claybourne offered them with gratitude. After assuring RaZiel that she could see to Ada's needs, Charmaine walked Ada to her room and made sure she was tucked in. She'd been about to leave when Ada reached out and grabbed her hand.

"Can you stay, just until I fall asleep?" Her niece's voice was so small, so unsure, Charmaine almost didn't recognize it. Thoughts of her own bed flew from her head immediately.

"Of course, I'll stay, dear. Whatever you need."

Ada nodded and pressed her lips together, trying to hold back tears. "This is the moment I've dreaded most. Falling asleep, then waking up and knowing she's not here. That she'll never be here again."

Charmaine smiled to fight back her own grief welling up underneath her thin veneer of calm.

"Her love is with us. That will never die. And one day, we'll see her again."

"If that's true, then why does Papa look like she's gone forever?"

Charmaine wasn't prepared to reveal something she was only just now beginning to understand, but her mind was too exhausted to finesse its way around an answer, so she told Ada the truth.

"Because for him, she is. Even with your power, he knows he will leave this realm, but I don't think that it's clear to him if that means he will see her again."

For a moment, Ada looked stricken, as if startled awake by a terrifying sound, before she settled into a sober revelation.

Charmaine shook her head, frustrated by her own lack of certainty on how to comfort her niece. "I didn't mean to upset you."

"You didn't. I mean, I knew already. It's just that sometimes I forget that as bad as this is for me, for us, in some ways it's even worse for him."

Charmaine settled into the small chair beside Ada's bed, holding her hand until they were both asleep.

Outside their door, RaZiel sat on the ground, back propped against the wall, legs splayed out in front of him. He didn't mean to eavesdrop on their conversation. He couldn't help his senses. His only intention was to stay close to the only two people he had left in the world as he let the sound of their heartbeats lull him into a restless slumber.

⚙ ⚙ ⚙

Apart from Charmaine making her way to her own quarters a few hours later, she and Ada slept the entire trip. By early morning the next day, the city of Kemet was in sight.

An hour before the Cypher touched down, RaZiel brought a tray of water, dried fruit, and bread to each of their rooms. He found Charmaine already up and preparing to disembark while Ada was still deep in sleep.

Silently, he set the tray down on Ada's small nightstand and smiled at his little girl. It had been a long time since RaZiel had woken Ada up. In the forest, she tended to get up on her own, but before then, when she was a child, it was his job.

Before he could stop himself, before he even knew what he was doing, RaZiel began to sing their morning song as he always did, in a tone only she could hear because it was a song for angels.

Ada opened her eyes slowly, blinking two times, just as she did when she was a child. The thought that he still knew this about her after all these years filled him with a quivering joy, and, as her eyes focused and found his, despite all the terrible things that had happened, she smiled back.

❁ ❁ ❁

Knowing that Charmaine St. James was as exacting a woman as her sister, Captain Claybourne followed her instructions to the letter, setting the Cypher down at the dock nearest to her privately owned and guarded shipyard, where she produced the weapons and tools she and Lilavois had worked on for years. Though he'd never been here before, he knew parts of the Cypher itself had been manufactured in this shipyard, and, as he extended his ship's landing gear, he couldn't help uttering another prayer of thanks for the many gifts Lilavois had brought to his life, not the least of which was introducing him to her sister.

Charmaine looked as sharp as always in yesterday's outfit, but the strain of the last few days was clear in the fading luster of her hair and the wilted ruffles of her blouse. Nonetheless, as soon as they were on the ground, Charmaine got right to business, ushering Ada, RaZiel, Captain Claybourne, and Kibuka to the front door of a large hangar guarded by four burly men. They did not smile at her approach but moved swiftly to the side as she drew near.

"Good morning, Aravis," Charmaine said warmly.

Aravis took a moment to clear the rasp from his throat before he replied. "Good morning, Ms. St. James."

"This is Captain Claybourne, my niece Ada, my brother-in-law RaZiel, and Kibuka, a friend of the family." Charmaine pointed behind her. "If any of these four—and only these four—approach this door, please allow them entrance and provide any assistance they require. Inform your unit of my instructions."

"Yes, Ms. St. James."

Charmaine proceeded to slide a four-sided key into the door, while the smallest of the guards slid another three-sided key into the lock above that one. They turned the keys in unison and the door unlocked.

"Thank you, Mysar," Charmaine smiled. "Be on your guard. We should expect trouble soon."

"Understood," Mysar replied before closing the door behind them.

Ada, RaZiel, Captain Claybourne, and Kibuka followed Charmaine through a tall corridor that obscured their view of a large open space until they were deeper inside the structure. When they finally made a sharp left, Ada gasped as the room opened up and the magnitude of Charmaine and Lilavois's endeavor became clear.

Lined in neat rows were weapons of every kind, from long barrel pistols to crossbows outfitted with obsidian and blue jade tips, canisters of obsidian gas, and metal shields with Adrinkra symbols glowing blue with mooncraft.

"I didn't think there was this much blue jade in the entire world," Captain Claybourne exclaimed.

Charmaine gave him a sly smile. "There is if you know where to look."

"What was all this for?" Ada asked.

"For you," Charmaine replied. "Your mother had it in her mind that if Saisho ever found you, she would arm all of Liren to defend you. We wanted to make sure we were ready."

"How long have you been working on this?" Captain Claybourne asked.

"As you know, some of these materials are very rare. It took time to find or grow everything we needed, but we began shortly after Lilavois settled in Liren."

"But there's more here than would be needed to arm every man, woman, and child in Liren," RaZiel noted. "Why did you continue?"

"That part was for you," Charmaine replied. "She thought if the Covenant was ever needed again, you might benefit from some better tools. There are four thousand of the Fallen in total. Even though most are not members of the Covenant, there is a weapon here for each and every one of you."

"And she was right," Ada whispered. Pride in her mother's vision brought tears to her eyes.

"Why did you tell the guards we should expect trouble soon?" Captain Claybourne asked.

"Because once the Fallen realize that we're able to reproduce and distribute Ada's power on a large scale, they will look to destroy our supply. Not just Ada, but anything she's enchanted. It won't take them long to trace the weapons from the Sisterhood back to any remaining family or refuge Ada might have, and that trail will lead them back to me."

Charmaine glanced at her watch. "The Sisterhood should have joined the fight in Bel Mar by now, with most of the weapons that were aboard the Cypher and their own arsenal distributed and in use. Bel Mar is another day and a half's journey from here by airship." Charmaine glanced at RaZiel. "Of course, demons move faster than an airship when they fly. My guess is we have maybe twenty-four hours to safely move these weapons and get you both back on the Cypher. Sixteen if we want to be especially careful, which I think we do. It's not safe for you to stay in one place too long."

"You've never met Obi, and yet you've figured out his plan better than he has, I'm sure!" RaZiel said, marveling at her quick thinking.

Charmaine gave him a devilish grin. "I know because I'm not nearly as amiable as I appear." Her smile fell as her expression became more serious. "It's what I would do if someone was trying to hurt you. I would track down every lead. I would kill any enemy to keep you safe—and if they're half as determined to maintain their power as I am to see us through this, then they should not be underestimated."

RaZiel nodded, still a bit in awe at finding a clear reflection of Lilavois's fierceness in her sister. He'd always known that Lilavois was close with her sister, that she trusted her implicitly despite their divergent paths, but he'd never had the opportunity to fully understand why until now.

"Ada, how long will it take you to enchant everything we have here?" Charmaine asked.

Ada looked around the room. Some of the weapons, like the obsidian gas canisters, were quite delicate, with elements she'd never worked with before. "I'm not sure. I'll need to move more slowly to make sure I don't break or trigger anything."

"I'll help you," RaZiel said. "Your mother and I built the prototypes for many of these weapons. I know how they work well enough to keep you safe."

"All right," Ada replied, feeling a bit more relieved. "Maybe four to five hours."

"Excellent. That will give us some wiggle room to refresh ourselves before your next journey."

"What about you?" Captain Claybourne added. "It won't be safe for you here either."

"Don't worry about me, darling," Charmaine replied with a wink. "I've always been hard to catch."

CHAPTER TWENTY-FIVE

FAULT LINE

With RaZiel's help, Ada was able to finish enchanting Aunt Charmaine's stockpile in just under four hours, leaving ample time for them and Captain Claybourne's entire crew to spend a few well-deserved hours in the confines of Charmaine's luxurious home.

When they arrived from the warehouse, Aunt Charmaine emerged freshly bathed and coiffed in black leather and silk with the scent of rose perfume trailing in her wake like a desperate lover.

"Welcome!" She smiled brightly despite the strain that still lingered in her eyes.

Ada noted that Hannibal, the boisterous and feral Pomeranian that she encountered during her last visit to Aunt

Charmaine's house, was sitting dutifully and quietly at her aunt's feet.

"We've had baths prepared for all of you," Charmaine continued. "Supper will be served in the dining room shortly after." She gestured to a sharply dressed man in a matching deep cream long sleeve shirt and trousers standing in the corner of the room. "However, if you'd prefer to dine alone, please let my butler, Allister, know. We'd be happy to set up dinner service in the comfort of your own rooms. This has been a difficult time. The days ahead will undoubtedly bring more hardship and sorrow. I encourage you to attend to your own needs as you prepare for what is to come."

At some silent signal, Allister left the corner and appeared at Charmaine's side. "Captain Claybourne, Allister will show you and your crew to your rooms. Ada and RaZiel, please come with me."

When Allister and the crew departed, Charmaine led Ada and RaZiel down the opposite hall from where Allister had taken the Cypher's crew to the guest bedrooms directly across from her own. When the door closed behind them, Charmaine rushed to Ada, taking her face between her palms.

"You're back sooner than I expected. Did everything go well? If you're too tired, we can make arrangements for you to work on simpler—"

"I'm fine." Ada replied. She eased Charmaine's hands from her cheeks then held them gently between them.

RaZiel rested a hand on Charmaine's shoulder. "Ada did well. She's become very efficient in her craft."

"It was easier working together," Ada added. "Aunt Charmaine, are you okay? I've never seen you so... anxious."

Charmaine let her hands fall away with a sheepish smile. "I'm fine, dear, but I'm sure you're tired. Don't let me keep you. Go and rest. We'll talk more before you leave. The washroom is just through there."

Something in her aunt's smile felt forced, but after everything they'd been through, Ada couldn't really blame her. They were all struggling, but what good would it do to linger on those thoughts now? Wasn't the grief enough?

"Thank you," Ada said, taking a moment to hug Charmaine before heading toward the hot water she knew was waiting for her.

RaZiel watched until Ada closed the bathroom door behind her before turning his attention back to Charmaine.

"Your rooms are connected so you can watch over her. Your bedroom is just there," Charmaine said, pointing to an open door on the right.

RaZiel sighed. "I know we don't know each other yet, but I can see you're not well. Have you slept?"

Charmaine couldn't control the trembling of her hands. "I... tried. I couldn't. I don't know how you and Lilavois did this."

"Did what?"

"Survived the constant worrying. I'm so scared for her

already I can barely breathe," Charmaine whispered as her eyes filled with tears. "I had no idea..."

Gently, RaZiel pulled her into his embrace. "You have to have faith," he whispered. "It's the only way you're able to let her out of your sight."

After a moment, Charmaine felt strong enough to stand on her own again.

"I do," she said, swiping away her tears. "I know that you and the Covenant will protect her. It's the only reason I'm able to let her go."

⚙ ⚙ ⚙

Dinner that night was a somber affair. While his crew took advantage of the time to rest in the privacy of well-appointed rooms, Captain Claybourne shared the information he and his crew had gathered over the course of the day through telegram communications with other airship captains who were aligned with the Sisterhood.

"It appears that the distribution of Ada's weapons didn't receive the rousing reception we hoped from some of the governments and citizens you'd think would be glad that the era of demons can finally come to an end. From the reports I'm getting, the introduction of Haven House's arsenal in Bel Mar was decisive. Within a few hours, the demons there were driven back or killed, but most importantly, even more demons are joining the Covenant to protect Ada."

Charmaine leaned forward with Hannibal perched securely on her lap. "So why isn't this good news?"

"Some of the demons who fled are now appealing to local governments, offering money and service for clemency."

Charmaine narrowed her eyes. "Since when has any demon submitted to government authority?"

"Apparently some are claiming that they're not part of Obi's clan of demons. They say they're being falsely targeted by the Sisterhood and the Covenant. They claim they just want to live in peace."

Ada frowned. "And people are believing them?"

"Some are. A few governments have called for a truce until an official policy can be put in place. In the meantime, others are demanding that the mooncraft behind these new weapons be turned over to authorities immediately."

"SeKet will not let this stand," RaZiel warned.

"That's good to hear," Captain Claybourne continued. "Because there are reports of demon attacks still happening in Java, Jericho, and Mendefera, but my sources say there are new attacks every day. The Sisterhood and the Covenant are responding to calls for help, but we'll need new weapons to arm them all."

"And who are these sources?" Charmaine asked.

"Captains I've gotten to know and trust over many years of flying routes together," he replied. "Most of us relied on your sister for medical training and supplies. When I told them what happened to her in Liren, most were pretty upset. But more than that, they've seen the devastation caused by the demons firsthand. Several had already signed on to help the Sisterhood as transports."

"But why would people believe the Fallen," Ada said, "when, after all this time, we can finally do something about them?"

RaZiel squeezed Ada's hand. "Because sometimes people believe the evil they know is safer than the uncertainty of building something new. In Liren, they were willing to side with Obi in exchange for their own safety, even if it meant you would suffer, even if it meant others would suffer. They weren't willing to lose what they had for the possibility of something else. Something that would be harder to obtain but perhaps more valuable—a chance to truly be free."

CHAPTER TWENTY-SIX

THE MISTAKE

Eighteen hours after they'd arrived in Kemet, RaZiel, Ada, and the crew boarded the Cypher headed to Mendefera.

As the Cypher lifted off for the four-hour journey, RaZiel and Ada stood by one of the craft's large windows holding each other as they watched Charmaine's waving silhouette fade into the distance.

When she was completely out of sight, RaZiel released Ada from his embrace to get a good look at his daughter. Her eyes were as sharp as her aunt's and as knowing as her mother's. Ada's hair was braided and swept away from her face in a style that made her look somehow both younger and more mature. Gone were the worn clothes she had when they arrived. In fact, her whole attire was new except for Lilavois' lasso, which hung from a belt around Ada's waist.

Ada wore a pair of thick, fitted purple pants embellished with gold thread and altered to fit neatly into Ada's prosthetic. Her matching vest was embroidered in heavy threads of orange and yellow with Adinkra symbols that RaZiel knew were meant for protection. All of this fit snugly over the fine cotton of a white blouse with a fluted collar that was unlike anything RaZiel had ever seen. Outside the tension in her shoulders and the shadows under her eyes, one might almost believe the last few days had never happened.

"You look very nice. Your aunt has exceptional taste."

Ada looked down at her outfit and shook her head. "I know. She had everything laid out for me when I woke up. I don't even know how she had all this made, much less tailored." Ada stuck her leg out. "She even had my boot and prosthetic polished! When I asked her how she had the time to do all this, she said, 'A woman must always be prepared for battle.' I'm not even sure I know what that means, but the fit of these clothes is perfect."

"I wouldn't be surprised if she has a team of seamstresses and tailors working around the clock," he chuckled before adding more seriously, "Are you sure you're ready for this? We have the weapons you enchanted. You don't need to be here."

Ada eyed him skeptically. "You don't either. We could just ask Captain Claybourne to deliver the weapons to the towns that want them and go home."

"Until I'm sure the Fallen have accepted you fully, you will never be safe, and I will never stop fighting until you are."

"And because you won't stop, you won't be safe either, which is why we're both here."

RaZiel gave her a knowing smile. "I'm glad to see your mother's stubbornness lives on."

They laughed together for a few moments before Ada fell silent, wandering to a nearby bench to sit down. At first, RaZiel felt sure his mention of Lilavois was the reason for Ada's sudden change in mood. He sat beside her for a while longer before lifting her chin.

"If it's too painful for me to mention her, I won't. It's just... for me, she is always in my thoughts. Every second of every day. It has been that way since I met her, and it will be that way beyond the end of time."

"I don't mind you talking about her. Mama deserves that." Ada touched her chest. "I miss her so much it hurts. Talking about her feels like keeping her with me. I need that."

"Then what's on your mind?"

Ada closed her eyes and began fiddling with her hands.

"I was thinking about Simon," she said softly. "Mama's gone, and he doesn't even know. He's the first person I would have talked to about it. He's my best friend."

RaZiel smiled. "I think he's more than that, no?"

Ada's eyes flew up to his as a bright burgundy blush hit her cheeks.

RaZiel chuckled. "Your mother and I did see you kiss him goodbye in Liren, remember?"

Ada covered her face and let out a muffled groan as RaZiel nudged her playfully with his elbow. "But more than that, I hear it in your heart when you speak of him. Love is nothing to be embarrassed about, especially when you're loved in return."

She dropped her hands and stared at him. "How could you know that?"

"Because I know the sound of a heart in love. Intimately. I would never have given you to him to look after in Bonn if he did not love you."

It took a moment for Ada to think back. "When I woke up, he was carrying me, but I couldn't remember how I got there." Ada's lips began to tremble as she fought to hold back the grief of this new knowledge. "But it doesn't matter. That's why I sent him away. It's not safe for him here. *I'm* not safe. To love someone means you keep them safe, even if it means sending them far away from you. Doesn't it?"

"I used to think so, but I don't anymore."

"What do you mean?" Her tears were coming too fast to wipe away. "You left to keep us safe."

"I did, but now, with your mother gone, I understand my mistake. When you were small, she tried to convince me to stay. She believed it was better to fight together than to be safe apart. I don't think she cared if we died. As a human, it's something you know will eventually happen. What I couldn't understand then, what I know now, is that she was willing to risk it to have the chance to *live* together. She wanted us to fight *together*.

"At the time, I thought that death was the worst thing that could happen to us, but it wasn't. I will lose you one day, just as I lost her, but before then, I can love you. I can live and fight with you. We can live before you die. All the time I lost with you, with her, I can never get back. I wasted it being so scared of death I forgot the blessing of living here and now with you. Seeing you grow up, hearing her laugh, feeling her touch. I would never make the same mistake again, and I don't want you to either. When this is over, find him and make sure you live before you die."

"But what if he's still mad? What if he won't forgive me?"

"I'm sure he's already forgiven you as your mother forgave me."

"How do you know?"

"Because he knows you love him too."

CHAPTER TWENTY-SEVEN

MENDEFERA

From the extent of the destruction on the ground it was clear that the fighting in Mendefera was heavier than the reports told. From the pilot's deck, Captain Claybourne looked down on the hundreds of demons and E'gida battling in the streets and the trail of demon and human remains in their wake.

Every once in a while, he saw a flash of sunlight amid the smoke and ash and realized that at least a few of Ada's weapons had made their way here from Bel Mar.

By the number of E'gida on the ground, it was clear that the airships had been successful in transporting their cargo. Getting out alive, however, seemed to present a bigger problem. Captain Claybourne noted the graveyard of ships, three by his count, scattered beneath him as he circled around the ravaged city for a safe place to land.

From the torn sails and claw marks that riddled the sides of each ship hull, it was not hard to guess what had brought each airship down. But that was the Cypher's biggest advantage: with Lilavois's mooncraft activated, the ship could fly unseen.

"Get ready!" he yelled to his crew. "We have to clear a spot to land."

"We can help," RaZiel replied, already holding one of the crossbows and a quiver of arrows that Ada had enchanted.

"Good. We need you and Magic Fingers to take the front guns."

Ada's mouth fell open in outrage, only to have her own father burst out in laughter at her side.

"Seriously?!" she exclaimed while losing the battle with her own smile.

"Don't sass your elders." Captain Claybourne smiled. "We'll work on your nickname later. Right now, there's a group of E'gida in front of us who could really use our help."

RaZiel, Ada, and the crew raced down to the Cypher's lower deck and took up their positions.

In front of them, three E'gida stood atop a mound of rubble, their lassos drawn and lashing out against a crowd of five demons who surrounded them. Any moment, they would be overrun.

The Cypher's crew fired, hitting the first three demons with ease. RaZiel's arrow hit the fourth. But by then, the fifth demon knew what to expect. It shifted to the left, avoiding the crew's arrows as it picked up a large piece of rubble and hurled it in the direction of the Cypher.

Captain Claybourne had positioned the airship closer to the ground than he would normally risk flying to give their weapons the best chance to reach their targets. There was no way he could maneuver away from such a large projectile in time to avoid it.

Seeing the large piece of metal and stone hurling toward them, Ada extended her hand, projecting her e'gida over the front of the ship. The rubble crashed against it, inches from the ship's front window, but never made contact. Her body shook as she felt the impact ripple through her, almost as if the rubble had struck her directly. Ada stumbled back before the mooncraft energy in her prosthetic flared, holding her in place and pulsing with enough strength to help her withstand the blow and maintain her e'gida.

Ada looked down at her leg and saw it shining brighter than it ever had, shimmering in a brilliant blue that cast its light across the entire lower deck.

Her mother's words from when Lilavois first gave her the prosthetic came back to her.

If anyone hits you, the leg is designed to push back with an equal and opposite force.

Beside her, RaZiel's eyes shone with fresh tears. "Even now, she is with you."

Ada nodded, unable to speak as she realized how much of

Lilavois's power still lived on in this ship, in her prosthetics, and in her.

Outside, the demon was furious that his attempts to bring down the ship were thwarted. He reached for another giant boulder, but before he could throw it, RaZiel pierced him with a golden arrow through his chest. Startled by the impact and the metamorphosis that had just begun, the demon buckled to his knees.

"Be at peace, Hermes," RaZiel whispered before reloading his crossbow.

In the pilot's seat, Captain Claybourne let out the breath he'd been holding before he used his foot to kick open the lip of the small porthole he used to communicate with the lower deck.

"What the heck was that?" he bellowed.

"Magic Fingers!" Ada yelled back with a smirk.

Captain Claybourne barked out a laugh. "Well, keep it up! There's plenty more where that came from."

Across the battlefield, word spread quickly that the demon slayers' weapons had made their way to Mendefera. Using their aerial advantage, the Cypher continued their attack, cutting the number of demons the E'gida had to fight in half.

Seeing the battle turn against them so quickly, those demons who could, fled, chased down and out of the city by a blade of light held in the hand of lightning itself. When the last of the demons had left, SeKet walked out of the dust and gloom and met the Cypher where it settled outside the city gates.

As soon as Ada stepped from the ship, SeKet embraced her.

"I'm so sorry, little one. Kibuka told me what happened. Your mother was a great woman."

"Thank you," Ada muttered, not wanting to let her emotions show in front of the crowd of E'gida who were gathered around them. "We came as quickly as we could."

Noticing the change in subject, SeKet studied Ada for a moment before nodding in silent understanding. There would be another place and another time to grieve.

"I see," SeKet smiled, looking from Ada to RaZiel, Captain Claybourne, and his crew. "We're most definitely in need. The authorities in Bel Mar seized most of the arsenal you sent to us."

They stared back in shock. "Why?" RaZiel asked.

SeKet sucked her teeth in disgust. "They've declared their lands to be neutral ground until a diplomatic solution to the conflict is reached. All the members of the Sisterhood were required to surrender everything we had in the field and any supply within the convents. As you can imagine, Jhonna is furious. She's still in Bel Mar trying to negotiate their return, but, of course, it's all a ruse. Obi has frightened them or paid them off somehow."

"How did you manage to leave with that sword?" Ada asked.

SeKet smirked. "Who would take it from me? As I told you, little one; no one wants to fight me. The entire Covenant left with whatever weapons we could carry."

Ada looked around, noticing Tlaloc, Al-Yah, and Heka within the crowd. "Where is the rest of the Covenant?"

"We've spread out, fighting the other attacks that Obi still has in play, but I suspect once the news that you've made more weapons reaches them, the rest of the Fallen, like those here, will flee."

"How many have we lost so far?" RaZiel said, conflict written on his face.

"Nearly five hundred kin. Most received mercy. Others are lost to us forever."

RaZiel reached out to hold SeKet's hand. "I'm sorry, Sister. I know the pain of this loss."

For a moment, SeKet eyes closed against the needless death she had seen. "I will not apologize for things I did not cause, and neither should you."

"Where will the Fallen go?" Captain Claybourne asked.

"To RaHabel," SeKet replied. "Obi will want to gather his strength now that the Sisterhood and the Covenant have united."

"How many stand with us in the Covenant?" RaZiel asked.

"We're three hundred and two, as of today." She smiled, nodding to their newest members.

"So many?" RaZiel gasped.

"Yet still not enough to end this conflict," SeKet sighed.

A short woman from the crowd of E'gida stepped forward. "But now that the truce has been called, the Sisterhood is of no use to you. Without weapons, we can't help you defeat them."

SeKet turned to her. "Sister Dawnetta, yes?"

The woman nodded. "You helped us escape a dead end where the Fallen would have killed us earlier today. Jhonna and I studied together at the convent in North Kesar. She sent a telegram urging us to come here and join forces with you."

"How many of you have come?"

"We've one hundred and fifty in our party, with more in Jericho and Java."

"And what of the other convents? If you sent word to them, do you think they would defy the ceasefire?"

"I do, but without a way to transport them safely, it won't matter."

"Did any of the transports survive?" Captain Claybourne asked, thinking of the three downed airships he saw earlier.

"None were as fortunate as you," Dawnetta replied. "After we disembarked, not a single ship could get high enough before the Fallen took them down. I've never seen an airship powered by mooncraft before, much less one that is invisible. Who designed your vessel?"

Captain Claybourne looked to Ada. Though they had been friends, the story of Lilavois's legacy was not his to tell. He found Ada looking back at the Cypher, apparently pondering the same thought.

"My mother, Lilavois St. James, did," Ada replied. "And you wouldn't have to be without weapons. We brought enough to arm everyone here. Are there members of the E'gida among you who are skilled blacksmiths and alchemists?"

Dawnetta frowned. "There are."

"Good. My mother left instructions on how to use mooncraft to enhance the Cypher's speed and shield it from view. I can share them with you so we can outfit other airships with the same capabilities."

"We would be grateful for the knowledge and the weapons you could provide those of us who are here." Dawnetta paused. "But unless there are enough to arm every E'gida who would join us, I'm still not sure how useful we would be against a horde of three thousand demons."

RaZiel looked at Ada, then Dawnetta, with a knowing smile. "If the Sisterhood is willing to break the ceasefire, we know someone who can provide all the weapons you'll need."

CHAPTER TWENTY-EIGHT

STOWAWAY

"Now, Hannibal, don't be difficult! In times of war, economies must be made."

Hannibal stared back at her from the deck of the Titan, unconvinced.

Charmaine chartered the steamer the day RaZiel and Ada left and had been sailing ever since. Though it was a far cry from her usual standards for accommodation, the ship served her purposes well. The crew kept their curious stares to a minimum while transporting goods from port to port, which enabled her to travel inconspicuously but on a predictable schedule where she could check for messages from Allister at every major port regarding if and where she might be needed. Most importantly, she could do all this while still smuggling the bulk of her weapons supply in a discrete lower deck that would never be discovered under routine inspection.

Even with the need for haste, she'd still managed to bring aboard a four-by-six pallet of grass that she'd designed specifically to address her beloved Pomeranian's outdoor needs. Hannibal had not been appreciative. Nonetheless, for Charmaine, defecating all over the deck was simply out of the question. Who knew how long they'd be on this ship!

"If I can use a chamber pot, you can use this pallet," she said sternly. "I will not ask again. Do your business!"

Resigned to his fate, Hannibal squatted with dignity.

Charmaine took her time walking back to her room. Beyond her trips to the local post office whenever they docked, most days she stayed tucked away inside the Titan's lower deck to avoid being seen. But at night, when the boat was out at sea, she could roam freely. Having been confined to cramped quarters for most of their three-day journey, the night air felt precious against her skin. Beyond the placid waves that lapped against the ship's hull, the sea felt gentle and ominous at the same time, as if she was completely at its mercy. Charmaine respected its power, as she respected her own.

Kenson Gerald, the owner of the fleet of cargo ships, had been a suitor many years ago, back in Charmaine's rebellious days when having a renowned pirate for a boyfriend seemed like a good idea. Though they parted ways due to a startling dispute over the proper way to bathe, they remained friends.

Over the years, he'd helped her locate many of the items she and Lilavois needed to build their weapons, and in return, she let him keep some of her more precious finds and paid him handsomely for his discretion. When she shared her need for a transport that could both disguise her mission and see it through, he'd volunteered his fleet without hesitation.

With its weathered planks and paint-chipped rails, the Titan was nothing much to look at. But, as with most good things, its real worth lay beneath the surface. The propellers and steam engine were built for speed and agile handling, even with heavy cargo. To the untrained eye, the crew looked like any other group of sailors, broad and fit, with only one or two exceptions. Only the assortment of knives, axes, and pistols at their belts would let you know they were well accustomed to putting up or putting down a fight.

Their task was to deter human interference. If anything supernatural found them, they had strict instructions to stand down and let Charmaine handle the situation personally. She didn't want anyone putting their lives at risk unnecessarily. Their instructions were simply to deliver the cargo.

While Hannibal stopped to chew on a particularly thick piece of rope, Charmaine touched the telegram resting inside her corset.

After docking in Amanpor this morning, she went to the post office and found a telegram waiting for her. As was her custom, Charmaine didn't read it immediately, though she always sent the same reply, *Love, Charmaine*, which told Allister that she was still alive and his message had been received. Afterward, she took her time, strolling the market square, gathering up the latest newspapers and listening to the local talk. While enjoying sips of her morning tea, she eavesdropped. In between the bartering and trading, the demon scourge was all that was on anyone's mind.

"Things were fine before the Sisterhood started attacking the demons. If they would just stay in their convents, none of this would have happened. All this ruckus is bad for business," complained a stout merchant with a heavy knot of hair tied at the nape of her neck.

"You forget this all started with the Stone Killings," her customer countered as he searched his satchel for the coin to pay for his bushel of crabs. "And now they're scared because the Sisterhood has found a way to kill them off. Good riddance if you ask me."

Outside the café nearest to the docks, the sound of Mahjong tiles clattering about the tables could be heard throughout the square. Inside, the patrons' gossip leaned more toward keeping score of the battles than examining any deeper meaning to the war.

"I heard the Covenant's got themselves an invisible ship! Had them demons running for their lives in Mendefera!" someone chuckled.

"Don't laugh too loudly! They could turn up here! From what the papers say, they're still counting the dead bodies in

Bel Mar, but there's more of them than the Covenant, I'll tell you that," his colleague replied.

While the facts were often muddled, the sentiments were crystal clear. Though many disliked the conflict, few truly appreciated the danger they were in if the Fallen were not defeated.

Charmaine returned to the Titan earlier than usual to read the telegram in private. Her hands shook as she read the coded message that told her the ship's routine voyage was about to take a drastic turn.

Reached the isles safely
Alice sends her regards
Here at least a fortnight
Before we take a ferry to Mora
Either way, promise to bring gifts
Let us know you're well

RaHabel. She and the Titan's crew would be bringing their entire arsenal to the Fallen's ancient lair.

Instinctively, Charmaine knew this would be their last stand, the place where they would succeed or never return. To his credit, when she informed the ship's captain of their destination, he did not flinch. The crew simply picked up anchor and set sail.

If everything went as planned, the Titan would reach the shores of Eden in two days.

That night, Charmaine fell asleep with her clothes on and Hannibal and her pistol resting on either side of her hip.

She woke to the sound of the captain screaming, "Take cover!" Seconds later, the walls of her cabin shook as something heavy landed on deck.

For once, Hannibal was too scared to bark. Slowly, Charmaine got to her feet and tucked him behind her pillow. Then, pistol in hand, she pressed her ear to the door to hear what transpired above.

"You're far way from shore, Captain. Have you not heard of the danger in these waters?" she heard one of the demons ask.

The captain's voice was raised, no doubt for her benefit, but steady as he delivered the lie they'd practiced in the event of an attack. "We're delivering a shipment of coffee and provisions to Rega."

"And the woman you have on board?"

The captain hesitated. "She paid for passage to visit relatives there."

"I know her scent," another demon with a lower pitch to his voice replied. "Bring her to us."

"We can't. She locks herself in her room at night for security. She has the only key."

Startled, Charmaine backed away from the door. Was the demon lying? Besides RaZiel, Kibuka, and a few other demons in Bonn, she hadn't encountered a demon since her father died.

There were only two possibilities. Either they'd been betrayed by one of the demons who came to Bonn, or—

Charmaine didn't need to finish the thought. Memories of broiling smoke, her father's blood flowing through her fingers, and his desperate gasps for air sprang to her mind, vivid and terrifying.

The gun twitched in her hand as she remembered the putrid color of the eyes that cut him down, then lingered before the E'gida came.

The rush of footsteps coming quickly snapped her attention back from the anguish of her past to the present. She wasn't that scared little girl anymore, and the captain had done exactly what he was told, leading them right to her.

They tore the door off its hinges in one swipe to find her waiting for them at the other side of her cramped quarters.

"There you are," Ayar smirked, standing before her in half-human, octopus form. "Aren't you a sight to behold? I see why Indra remembers you so fondly."

Charmaine narrowed her gaze and kept her pistol behind her back. "A gentleman wouldn't barge into a lady's room uninvited."

His grin widened. "I am no gentleman."

"That's a shame."

Before he could complete his first step, Charmaine brought her pistol out and fired two of Ada's enchanted bullets straight into his left eye and chest. The roar that erupted from him was deafening, but not enough to make Charmaine shift her stance.

As he fell, another demon ran forward, anguish on his face as he looked to Ayar on the ground.

She fired again. While he dodged the first bullet, the second grazed his cheek, which was all that was needed for the transformation to begin. He howled in pain as he sank to the ground beside his kin.

Charmaine allowed herself a moment to breathe before wondering whether it was truly over. She didn't have to wait long.

The first tendrils of shadow slithered through the air so swiftly she didn't see them until they coiled around her wrists. With a vice-like grip, they shook the gun from her hand and drove her back against the cabin wall.

It was only then that the billows of smoke she remembered from her childhood came fully into view. The glow of his eyes was worse than she remembered as the shadow crossed over the bodies at her threshold and fixed her with eyes that burned a sickly yellow. Dark gray and black shadow filled the room in an instant, crawling up her body like a thousand tiny fingers. Charmaine felt the cuts in her wrists as she struggled against the demon's hold, but though she could not get away, she refused to give in.

Darkness crowded around her neck and face, pressing in so close that Charmaine feared she would suffocate.

"Where are they?" a low voice growled. His gaze hovered so high above her she had to strain her neck to meet it, but she would not cower.

"I won't tell you."

"You have no care for your own life or the lives of the men aboard this ship?"

"And you would show us mercy? Is that why you're here?"

"If you submit to us, things can be as they were. There will be peace again. Give us the weapons and the demon child."

When Charmaine said nothing, the shadow tightened around her ribs painfully, forcing the air from her lungs.

"You've grown lovelier than I imagined you would. I had planned to take you for my own all those years ago, but the E'gida spoiled our plans."

"Is that how you would bring peace?" Charmaine gritted out through painful breaths. "By forcing young girls into submission? You killed my father! I would have died before I ever came with you."

Slowly, the smoke pulled back, easing the pressure around her ribs so she could breathe. Yellow eyes melted into warm brown as the head and torso of a man with burnished skin the color of dark cinnamon emerged. His black hair was thick as it flowed over his shoulders in ebony waves. His wide eyes were balanced perfectly with a curvaceous mouth and a high-bridged nose that flared out in sharp edges at the nostrils. He was, Charmaine thought begrudgingly, one of the most beautiful creatures she'd ever seen.

"I would not have needed to force you to do anything."

Indra lifted his hand to trace a cold talon down the flawless skin of her cheekbone. "All my prey come to me willingly."

Staring over his shoulder, it took Charmaine less than a second to make up her mind. If there was a chance she didn't have to die tonight, she would gladly take it. She met Indra's gaze with a slow smile, then let her eyes roam over his face and torso with obvious appreciation.

"I believe you," she purred. The bands of shadow fell away from her wrists.

"Then you'll give me what I want."

"Darling, a woman like me doesn't just give you what you want," Charmaine whispered, reaching up to cup his head in both hands. Slowly, she brought his mouth close to hers, as if drawing him in for a kiss. "We give you what you deserve."

Charmaine fell back against the wall, bracing her elbows against Indra's chest to absorb the impact of the broken arrow Simon drove into his back.

His knees buckled with the shock of the pain. "You can't defeat me," he wheezed.

"I just did," Charmaine replied before shoving him to the floor in disgust.

"Simon!" she gasped, stepping forward to hug him fiercely. "Thank God! How? What are you doing here?"

"I snuck onto the boat three days ago when you left Kemet."

"Why didn't you come to me?"

"I... I wasn't sure you wouldn't kick me off. When I heard

about Ms. Lilavois, I came to Kemet to ask for your help in finding Ada. When I got to your house, I saw everyone leaving. I figured you would meet up with them at some point, so if I followed you, I'd eventually get back to her."

"How did you get that arrow? The weapons below are sealed."

"I brought it with me from Bonn. When I left, I knew I would be back, so I took a few with me, just in case I ran into trouble."

Charmaine smiled. "I'm grateful for your help, truly, but you could have been killed. We're headed to RaHabel. It will only get worse from here."

"You're going."

"This is my family."

Simon paused, looking down at his bare feet. "It's my family too. Ada is my family."

Charmaine brought him back into her embrace. "Then I suppose I have no choice but to let you stay."

When she stepped back, the look of relief on Simon's face made her laugh. "And where are your shoes, young man?"

"It's easier to sneak around on a ship without them."

"Well, enough of that," Charmaine chided. "Let's find the captain so we can get the crew to throw these bodies overboard and check on the other vessels."

"You have other ships carrying weapons?"

Charmaine winked. "Come now, you can't imagine I, of all people, would put all my eggs in one basket?"

CHAPTER TWENTY-NINE

BARGAIN

Obi hated entering the council chamber. SeKet had ruined the space for him forever. Though the Fallen's sacred hall had been cleared of all debris, the hole she created could never be repaired. Instead, it stood as a constant reminder of the ruin that RaZiel had brought to them all.

Beside him, Vishin paced. "Ayar, Eros, and Indra should have been back by now. Something is wrong."

Obi grunted in frustration. Of course something was wrong.

Lucifer, the brother who had led them to this barren place, was behind the creation of the Sisterhood, the very organization whose sole mission was to defeat the Fallen—his own kin. The same Sisterhood that would train a young woman to wield her mooncraft with incredible power. The same young woman who would come to love one of their own and, through God's blessing, bear a child who could destroy them all.

Obi bristled at the thought that long ago, he and RaZiel had been inseparable.

"Did you hear me?" Vishin asked.

"Where are the others?" Obi replied.

"They're resting."

"How many have come?"

Vishin could not hold his gaze. "Not all. So far only two thousand eight hundred and seventy-nine have returned."

Obi felt the terror of the unknown between them. Were the others dead, or had they gone into hiding?

"Perhaps Ayar, Eros, and Indra fled with the others," Vishin offered.

"You don't believe that any more than I do. If they are lost to us, then there is nothing more to be done."

"Is that what you'll say when I'm gone? Not a word of remembrance or remorse?" Vishin shook his head. "What has happened to you?"

"You've read the papers, heard it confirmed by our own kin. Lucifer began the Sisterhood! RaZiel's own child has turned her power into a thousand swords against us. Even if the truce holds with Bel Mar and the other nations, we will always have to give more to defend it until we're spent, until we have lost everything we've built!"

"Haven't we already lost everything?" Vishin asked

quietly. "We were once angels, Obi. God's own. Do you remember what it felt like not to need or want *anything*? They worshiped us. Now, they call us demons. Can what the child offers truly be worse than what we've already suffered?"

Obi closed his eyes to breathe in the bitterness of the truth. Though none had said as much aloud, he'd sensed the doubt, the fear, the weariness in every one of his kin who returned. The idea that their dominance was no longer worth the price had taken hold.

"Do you no longer believe in our dominion here, brother?" Obi asked.

"I'm prepared to defend it with my life," Vishin replied, "if only because it's all we have left, but even I can admit losing it won't be the worst thing we've endured."

"We'll find out soon enough. Our spies report a gathering of airships in Java."

"How many?"

"Ten. But not all lands are allies. There could easily be more we don't know about. At least we'll see them coming."

"We didn't in Bonn," Vishin replied.

They stared back at each other with nothing left to say.

CHAPTER THIRTY

EDEN

The Cypher reached the shores of Eden at the southern tip of the peninsula in the middle of the night. SeKet had been right in anticipating Obi's next move. As soon as the Fallen retreated, they destroyed the closest train station to RaHabel in the city of Rega, effectively cutting off the valley's main route in or out of the region. But that wouldn't stop the fleet of airships that would arrive within hours.

Ada sat on the shore, watching RaZiel walk out of the ocean barefoot with a soaked shirt and trousers. Not wanting to call attention to their location, he decided to swim around the peninsula in search of Charmaine's vessel. On land, Ada knew he was fast, but in the water he was even faster, traveling miles in only a few minutes. Despite his ragged clothes, as he emerged from the water, even she had to acknowledge her father looked like a god.

RaZiel smiled as he walked up to her on the beach. "Your aunt is a wonder."

"What has she done this time?"

"She brings many treasures," RaZiel replied with a knowing smile. "I thought she'd only brought one ship, but instead she's commandeered three, each coming to shore from a different direction."

"Are you worried Obi will see?"

"RaHabel is a good distance from here and your aunt is well equipped to handle any demon who comes her way. Besides, they know we're coming. When they face your weapons again, they will want to do it with their full strength. Her fleet should be here within the hour."

Ada yawned as she watched the sky begin to lighten. She couldn't remember how long she'd been up, but her eyes burned and her leg was beginning to ache.

"We have a few hours before all the airships arrive. You should go back to the Cypher and get some rest while you can. It's a long trip to RaHabel."

"I remember," she said. "What will you do?"

RaZiel shrugged. "Pray." Something about the way Ada smiled at his words pleased him deeply. "Do you pray, Ada?"

"Sometimes, but not like you. Mama used to say that prayer isn't something you need to stop and do. It's a never-ending conversation. You just start talking with God and you never stop."

As she watched the slow smile spread across RaZiel's face, it occurred to her that she was talking with one of the few people who would actually know.

"Is that true?" she asked.

RaZiel stared for a moment, watching God shine in and through her in ways he could never explain. "It may be the best description I've ever heard. Everything you touch, everything you do can be prayer, if your intention is behind it."

"Then why do you kneel on the ground?"

"Because I like the feel of it beneath me. It forces me to listen more deeply to the heartbeat of the world. It reminds me of what it used to feel like to have God's voice with me at all times."

"You miss it."

RaZiel turned his eyes to the ocean, watching the waves break then disappear in the sand. "Only your mother eased the ache of it. Now, I've lost them both." He shook his head. "Go rest. I'll send someone to wake you when it's time."

✾ ✾ ✾

Charmaine and the two other boats arrived with the first of the airships.

They wasted no time arming every member of the E'gida from every convent that had answered Jhonna's call—two thousand in all. Under Charmaine's direction, there were enough to give each member and the Covenant as many weapons as they could comfortably carry and still have spares.

Given that the Fallen were likely expecting their approach, they decided their best chance was to attack from every side. Kibuka and Al-Yah and the newest members of the Covenant from Obi's court drew maps for each unit detailing RaHabel's secret entrances and pathways.

"But do your best not to attack unless it is absolutely necessary," SeKet directed.

"What do you expect us to do?" Jhonna said incredulously. "Ask to be invited for tea?"

"Ask them to join you in the council chamber. Tell them you seek an audience there."

"And what if they decide to kill us first?"

SeKet sighed. "Then do what you must, but understand this: you've come here to defeat your enemy. I've come here to save my family. We have been together longer than you can possibly fathom. We have never fought against each other as we are now. Never, because despite everything, we are all we have on this earth. We bear the same pain. We have the same memories. We know peace, even if some of us refuse to choose it."

"Then why do this?" Jhonna asked. "Why help us defeat your own kind?"

"Because we still remember who we once were, and no one else should have to pay for the mistakes we have made," RaZiel answered. "That is not why we were brought into being."

"RaZiel and I will try to speak to Obi and the council one last time," SeKet continued. "If they will not see reason, then we will end this. One way or another."

❈ ❈ ❈

"Wake up. It's time to go."

Ada felt sure she was dreaming. She could feel Simon's slim fingers tracing lightly over her forehead as he beckoned her awake.

She turned into his touch. "I miss you," she murmured.

Simon's hands stilled, stunned by the way her words mended the ache in his heart. Then he laughed. "Of course you do," he said. "I'm your best friend."

It was the laugh that brought her fully awake. No dream could capture the rolling timbre of his quietest, most private laugh or the way it made her skin tingle with anticipation.

Ada opened her eyes to find him smiling at her. "Simon! What are you doing here?"

"Where else should I be?"

"You shouldn't be here! We're going back to—"

He took her hand. "Here. Right here next to you is exactly where I belong."

"Simon." Ada looked down at where his hands covered hers, trying to tamp down the emotion welling in her eyes. "It's too dangerous."

"I love you, Ada," he said simply.

The admission surprised her so much she forgot to hide her reaction. She met his gaze with tears falling down her cheeks.

"I don't want you to get hurt because of me," she said. "You're supposed to protect what you love. I'm supposed to keep you safe."

"Do you love me, Ada?"

The thought of how much she did, how afraid she was to lose him, made it hard to speak. She nodded emphatically through her tears.

"Then don't lock me away. Keep me close so we can protect each other."

Slowly, he brought their lips together, and this time, she did not pull away.

CHAPTER THIRTY-ONE

SANCTUARY

Some climbed, and others flew, infiltrating the fortress of RaHabel at every doorway, the Sisterhood and the Covenant working together. Only RaZiel, Ada, SeKet, Kibuka, Charmaine, and Simon traveled back the way they'd come a few short months ago. While the others found no resistance along their secret pathways, SeKet encountered exactly what she expected. They touched down in the center of the council chambers to find Vishin, Obi, and Gaida waiting for them in front of a host of her kin.

"So you've come to finish what you started," Obi said.

"We've come to talk," SeKet replied. "To negotiate an end to this conflict and bring redemption for all those who seek it."

"Redemption? Is that what you call killing hundreds of your own kind?" Vishin asked. "Violating our sacred vow to each other to protect humans!"

SeKet shook her head. "We were created to love, Vishin. My strength, our strength, was given to protect those who can't protect themselves—even if it means standing against my kin."

"That duty was forsaken the moment we were cast down," Obi spat.

"We were not forsaken, brother," RaZiel replied. "The decision to leave was ours."

"Do not speak to me!" Obi roared. "You, who betrayed us over and over again!"

"Enough, Obi!" Gaida sighed. "SeKet, we once served in the Ever's guard together. We were kin. You come here with weapons but say you want to negotiate. What is your true purpose?"

"It is as I've said, but you should not expect me to come to this place defenseless. None of us are who we once were. It is time for this scourge to end. We will not stand by while you terrorize these people, not when Ada offers us a choice, a way to free ourselves from this misery."

"Speak for yourself!" Gaida said, her voice rising over her superior posture. "We came here to rule, not to cower with the humans." She paused to give Charmaine, Ada, and Simon a condescending glare. "And certainly not to become them."

Charmaine tapped the first gun on her belt and winked.

"Then you will die here," SeKet said sadly.

"As will you," Vishin replied. With a wave of his hand, the horde behind him rushed forward, but not before Obi lunged at RaZiel, and Charmaine fired her first shot straight into the center of Gaida's skull.

The chaos around them was instant as a horde of demons rushed forward, some in human and others in animal form. To Ada's right, Obi and her father were locked in a whirlwind of motion that made it hard for her to see what was happening, much less help. In front of her, SeKet and Kibuka were doing their best to take on the entire mob themselves, diverting each attack with a long swing of their swords. Standing in their wake, Charmaine wielded a gun in each hand as she picked off demons on the periphery. Slowly, Charmaine worked her way to the amphitheater seats, where she established a high ground position that gave her the best perspective on the battle.

From where she stood, their success was a long shot at best. Risking a glance behind her, she saw Ada and Simon working together with their crossbows to deflect any attack. With the bodies piling up around them, Charmaine could see they would soon be snared in a trap of their own making.

"Simon! Ada!" Charmaine yelled, using her gunfire to clear a path for them. "Get up here! Now!"

Ada nodded, moving first, while Simon followed, which was how she saw the demon coming up behind Aunt Charmaine. With no hope of reaching her in time, Ada reached out her hand and summoned her power to pierce him through.

Shocked, Charmaine turned around in time to see him fall down the stairs as his transformation began.

"Thank you, dear girl," Charmaine exhaled as Ada and Simon came up beside her. "Whatever that thing is that you just did, forget the crossbows and do *that* while Simon helps me reload these guns! I'm down to my last two full barrels. Unless the others arrive soon, the odds are not in our favor."

"SeKet and Kibuka seem to be keeping them at bay for now at least," Simon offered.

"'For now' is the operative phrase," Charmaine replied. "But there are only maybe a hundred here. What happens when the other demons arrive?"

Instead of answering, Simon began reloading her guns from the long pouch of bullets at her hip.

"And I can't find Papa," Ada said. "I lost him in all this mess."

"Your father can take care of himself," Charmaine replied, keeping her eye on the demons in front of them as she reached for the newly reloaded gun that Simon handed her. "Focus on keeping yourself alive until he's finished dealing with that wretch, Obi."

Despite the conflict in her heart, Ada couldn't deny her aunt's logic. From the elevated steps of the amphitheater, it was clear that SeKet and Kibuka were slowly whittling down the horde. They moved through it with a methodical precision while Aunt Charmaine's bullets, Ada's fire, and Simon's crossbow worked on the perimeter. Bodies in varying

phases of death and transformation littered the hall. It was
both a strangely beautiful and terrifying sight to behold. If the
rest of the Covenant and the Sisterhood arrived before the
other demons, there might be a chance.

The crowd had thinned to only a dozen demons when a
roar from across the amphitheater shook the room. Ada hadn't
seen from where Vishin had come, but as he lashed out, he
grabbed SeKet by the hair and flung her against the stone
wall. She crashed against it with such force that the impact
radiated across its surface. Dazed by the impact, SeKet sank
to her knees until Vishin grabbed her by the gold lapel of her
tunic and dragged her upright.

From the other side of the room, Ada felt SeKet hit the
wall like a stone in her chest. She could just make out Vishin's
twisted expression as he drew back his claws, the tips
gleaming with demon venom. For the first time, Ada saw the
fear of utter annihilation in SeKet's eyes.

"You're never going back," Vishin hissed. "None of us are."

The motion of his hand was a blur. Too fast for Ada to
see, much less react to, but her mind reached out regardless,
sending her E'gida forward in an age-old longing to protect, to
care, to save the ones you love.

His claw descended, meeting the impenetrable surface of
Ada's will. Eyes seething with rage, Vishin turned toward her.
Ada felt her power surging beneath her fingertips. This time,
she was ready.

But someone else got there first. The crack of Jhonna's

lasso sounded in the hall a moment before it wrapped around Vishin's neck. Even with the tiniest cuts around his neck, the braided leather was saturated with enough of Ada's power to begin the change. From behind Ada's e'gida, SeKet's shoulders sagged with relief.

"You will return, brother," she whispered. "And remember yourself again. God willing, one day, I will join you."

⚙ ⚙ ⚙

Charmaine let out a sigh of relief as the rest of the Covenant and the Sisterhood entered the hall.

"Thank goodness! We were afraid the Fallen had overwhelmed you. What took you so long?"

Jhonna struggled to find the words for what she had witnessed. "We encountered the Fallen," she began. "But not as we expected."

"How do you mean? Did they go into hiding?"

"Not exactly. Al-Yah and RaZiel spoke to them."

Ada stepped forward. "You saw my father? I lost track of him in all the fighting. Where is he?"

"He's with Obi in the sanctuary." Something in Jhonna's tone frightened Ada.

"Is he alright? What's happened?"

"He's asking for you. Please, come with me."

CHAPTER THIRTY-TWO

LAST RITES

The moment Vishin declared war, RaZiel knew what would happen. He had his weapon in hand, and yet he could do nothing but brace himself for impact as Obi barreled toward him with crazed malice.

The last time RaZiel was in this chamber, he'd been ready to kill. His only thought had been to protect Ada. Nothing else mattered. Obi's eyes had been vicious as he stabbed him through, but at least there had been some sense of sanity within his cruelty. The Obi rushing toward him now was different, yet strangely familiar. It brought him back to a burning village long ago and his first sight of the creature with long claws and sharp, bloodstained teeth that Obi had become.

Ethyne was the first time he saw Obi this way. At the time, RaZiel was too consumed with his own anger at who the

Fallen had chosen to be to comprehend what he was seeing. The second time, the choice to save his daughter's life overshadowed any other concern. But this time, with the loss of Lilavois so near, RaZiel finally understood the look in Obi's eyes for what it was. The hunger, the loneliness, the ache of being so broken had driven him mad.

When Obi's body collided with his, RaZiel embraced him fully. Pinning Obi's arms at his side to keep his talons secured, he guided them out of the room and to the one place he might be able to bring his brother back: the sanctuary the Fallen had created when they first arrived.

"Let go of me!" Obi roared. "Betrayer!"

RaZiel screamed as Obi used his teeth to tear at his shoulders and neck, but instead of letting him go, RaZiel held on tighter.

"I will not leave you again," RaZiel grunted as he picked Obi up and ran through the stone halls he'd once called home.

"Liar!" Obi hissed as he thrashed in RaZiel's arms. "I hate you!"

"I love you," RaZiel whispered back, remembering the soft red sand and the high wind-worn walls of the sanctuary cavern, the beauty of the rust-colored stone, the trickle of water that fell from deep underground pools hidden within the depths of the cave.

By the time the sanctuary was in sight, RaZiel's left

shoulder was almost torn to shreds, but he resolved to bear his wounds as Obi had borne his madness.

"Just a few feet more," RaZiel groaned as he pressed on.

When they arrived at the sanctuary entrance, RaZiel was in too much pain to hear anything clearly, which was why he stepped into the doorway without realizing that this was also the place where the Fallen had come to die.

They walked in to find Al-Yah and the other members of the Covenant pricking their kin with the sharp end of Ada's enchanted daggers. Behind them, Jhonna, Dawnetta, and the rest of the E'gida bowed their heads in respect as witnesses to these sacred last rites.

Instantly, RaZiel thought of SeKet and how much she had worked and suffered for this moment—to see her kin reach for the hope of redemption. Because Obi had grown still in his arms, RaZiel hoped that Obi too had felt the peace of this place, the sacred moment of surrender so many of his kin had chosen. He loosened his grasp, setting Obi on his feet. RaZiel kept a light hold on his hand as he walked toward Jhonna.

"How did this happen?" he whispered.

"They were waiting for us as soon as we entered," Jhonna began. "In different groups, at different locations. At first, we thought they would attack, but instead they wanted to talk. We thought it was a trap, but they never asked us to disarm. After Al-Yah and the other members of the Covenant spoke with them, we followed. They took us here. They said it was where they'd taken refuge when they first came here. Once we were inside, they asked us questions.

"They wanted to know if death would be swift, what it meant to die as a human. They wanted to know if the pain would be eternal. Of course, most of their questions we couldn't answer, but what we could, we did." Jhonna paused. "They told us that most of them had fought at Obi's command, believing that Ada's power was another kind of mooncraft designed to trap them in human form. But then they began to hear the reports from Bonn. Some saw the bodies, the faces of their kin who in death finally seemed closer to something they hadn't known for a long time—peace. The more they saw in Bel Mar, in Java, in Mendefera, the less they believed Obi. They brought us to the sanctuary to give them peace as well. Out of respect, we let the Covenant lead."

"Have they all...."

"Most, yes. Al-Yah and the others are almost finished."

In his joy, RaZiel squeezed Obi's hand, then let it go as he turned to him. "You see, Obi—"

RaZiel felt the tremor in Obi's body but did not understand what was happening until Obi broke free. Just like in Ethyne, his eyes suddenly turned crimson, and his teeth grew as long, narrow, and sharp as the talons on his fingertips.

RaZiel sprang forward to restrain him, but he did not reach him in time.

"No!" RaZiel screamed as Obi unleashed his rage.

Though he feared the Sisterhood would be most vulnerable, Obi attacked the Covenant first, killing Al-Yah and seven others in the blink of an eye before the Sisterhood could even begin to fight back.

"Leave Obi to me!" RaZiel told Jhonna before crashing into Obi a moment before he could sink his claws into another member of their kin.

"Find Ada!"

CHAPTER THIRTY-THREE

REMEMBERING PEACE

When Ada entered the sanctuary, the room was quiet save for the trickle of water that could still be heard over the snaps and growls that echoed off the cavern walls. Her eyes fixed on her father standing in the middle of the room with his arms wrapped around a feral demon. If there was anything to discern within the demon's snarls, the foam filling his mouth obscured his words. Yet all of that was secondary to the strain she saw on RaZiel's face as he tried to hold back this creature.

"Papa," she said gently, drawing closer.

"Stay where you are," RaZiel grunted. "He's already killed so many."

"What can I do?"

"Free him."

Ada looked around the room, where thousands of demons

lay dead, serene in their final resting places. Her father had not known this peace for four thousand years, but asked her to grant it to Obi while he lingered here without his kin or the one person who made his existence bearable.

Could she do it? Kill her own father to set him free? With shame, Ada realized that the one person who was born to answer his silent prayer never could.

With a nod, Ada raised her hand.

"Get away from me!" Obi hissed. "Don't touch me with your poison."

"Hear me, brother," RaZiel said. "This is my child! I want you to see her, Obi, truly see her! She is the answer to our pain, the answer to our prayers. Can you see her, Obi? She is proof that Abba has not forgotten us. Despite everything, God loves us still. Trust her as you once trusted me! She will see you home."

"You left me!" Obi cried. "We spent eternity together and then you left me here alone!"

"I'm sorry, Obi," RaZiel said, holding him so tightly his arms shook. "I'm sorry I didn't know how to bear this sorrow with you. Please forgive me, Obi! But I'll make it right. I'm trying to make it right."

Ada summoned her magic and released it as gently as she could into Obi's chest.

With a sigh of relief, RaZiel loosened his grip, shifting his body to see his brother one last time. "Be at peace, Obi," he whispered.

Slowly, Obi reached up. "There is no peace," Obi cried, piercing his talon through RaZiel's neck. "Without you."

"No!" Ada screamed as she dove to the floor, catching RaZiel's body as it fell.

Stunned, he reached for her, gripping her arm with fingers that already felt as light as dust.

"Ada," he whispered as translucent fluid leaked from the wound. "Tell your mother..."

"No," she said, placing her hand over his neck. "Tell her yourself." Urgency rippled through her as she poured her power into him with such force it lit the room.

Fighting the demon poison was like trying to fill a chasmic void with light. She could sense the pull like a bottomless hunger, sucking everything RaZiel had been out of him. Yet as she fought, a strange calm replaced her fear. The feeling was vaguely familiar. She struggled with the thought until she could place it. She had fought her own battle with demon poison long ago, yet only now did she truly understand what had happened. Even as a child, her power had been present enough to push back against the darkness, which meant that not only had she done it before and succeeded, she could do it again. Like Ada, her father would not survive unscathed, but that was not her goal. The demon in him would be sacrificed until only the man remained.

She could feel the abyss yield to her as she yielded back, letting it consume the parts of him he no longer needed while her own power transformed him.

In her arms, RaZiel gasped, his eyes wild and strangely uncertain as he felt the shift. Suddenly, his body began to convulse as a searing pain rippled through his neck. For the first time in his life, he coughed up blood.

With a sob of relief Ada closed her arms around him and cried. "You'll be alright now," she said. "Until I see you again."

"But what if I don't?" RaZiel rasped. "What if we never..."

Ada held him tighter. "We will," she cried. "If there is a way back to us, I know you'll find it."

RaZiel's smile was slow as he closed his eyes to the wonder of death. "I will," he whispered before kissing his daughter's hand goodbye.

For a long while, RaZiel's soul lingered, watching Simon wrap his arms around his beautiful child while he sang a lullaby Ada could no longer hear.

EPILOGUE

WHAT REMAINS

Lilavois and RaZiel watched her from the trees. Blew past her in the wind, then lingered like the smell of honeysuckle over the sound of her laughter.

Though years had passed, the sound of Ada's innocence had not changed.

Simon leaned in to brush his lips over her brow. "Are you teaching today?"

Ada caressed his jaw. Kissed him soundly. "Yes," she whispered when she was done. "I have to leave soon."

"Then, I'm coming with you. I can work on my book until you're finished."

"The Convent doesn't allow men," she teased, rolling their bodies so she was on top of him on their blanket in the grass.

"I'm not men. I'm yours."

Their little girl was now almost 30. A professor of

astronomy and a world-renowned demon slayer, but mostly, she was a woman who had ushered in a new era in human history—an age without the dominance of demons.

The Fallen were not all gone, but their numbers and the weapons she created had forced most into hiding, or at least cooperation with the human world. Either way, their presence was no longer Ada's concern. After they burned the bodies in the Sanctuary, she, along with Simon, Aunt Charmaine, the members of the Covenant who remained, and the Sisterhood walked out of RaHabel and did not look back.

Aunt Charmaine took Ada and Simon home to Kemet, and with SeKet's help, watched over them as they completed school and went to university. Ada studied astronomy, while Simon studied art history.

They married the day after they graduated and made Everland their home. Between frequent visits by SeKet, Aunt Charmaine, and Captain Claybourne, and their own travel for Simon's well-sought-after travel guides, Ada taught. Though Ada refused to join the Sisterhood, which had broadened its mission to a deeper study and application of mooncraft, she taught there in the summer months. During the rest of the year, she travelled to other universities throughout the world, sharing her insights on the make-up of the universe.

But what they didn't know was that with every discovery, Ada was merely looking for her parents, charting the Ever and imagining where in the vast universe they might be.

This pleased Lilavois and RaZiel the most, to know that she was seeking them as they always sought her.

They watched as Ada pulled Simon to his feet.

"Alright then, if you insist. The convent has given me a small office to use for the summer. You can work there until my lecture is over."

"But what if I want to listen in?" Simon teased. He gathered their blanket, then threw his arm around her shoulder.

"Oh my god! You've heard me ramble on about it for days already."

"But I like your rambling. It's good background noise for when I'm writing my books."

Ada's eyes narrowed. "What did you say?" Simon ducked down, just in time to avoid the swipe to his head.

"It was a compliment of sorts," he grinned. He stepped backwards as she picked up her skirt, preparing to pounce.

Without another word, he turned and ran, but not too fast, because the point was never to run away.

Ada wanted to catch him, and Simon would never miss the chance to be caught.

ACKNOWLEDGMENTS

This one was harder than usual. Life really tried me. I want to thank all my readers for always being patient with me— from the first book to the last.

To my editors, Jess, Michelle, and Tyler. Thank you. I know I asked a lot of you. I'm so grateful you delivered! To my design crew, Jocelyn and Jesse. Thanks for seeing my vision and lending your talent to it.

To my family and friends, thank you for your continual love and belief in me. I never take it for granted.

And finally, to God, for entrusting me with another story to tell. I am so blessed.

ABOUT THE AUTHOR

National bestselling and award-winning author Cerece Rennie Murphy has published thirteen speculative fiction novels, short stories, and children's books, including her latest release, In The Garden of Light and Shadow: War of the Fallen. Ms. Murphy is also the founder of Virtuous Con, an online sci-fi and comic culture convention that celebrates the excellence of BIPOC creators in speculative fiction. Ms. Murphy has received numerous awards, including the Science Fiction Writers of America (SFWA)'s Kate Wilhelm Solstice Award for significant contributions to the science fiction, fantasy, and related genres community. To learn more about her upcoming projects, please visit her website at www.cerecerenniemurphy.com.

instagram.com/cerecermurphy
tiktok.com/@cerecermurphy

ALSO BY CERECE RENNIE MURPHY

<u>The Wolf Queen Duology (Fantasy)</u>

The Wolf Queen: The Hope of Aferi

The Wolf Queen: The Promise of Aferi

<u>The Order of The Seers Trilogy (Science Fiction)</u>

Order of the Seers (Book 1)

Order of the Seers: The Red Order (Book 2)

Order of the Seers: The Last Seer (Book 3)

Between Two Seas (Short Story Collection)

To Find You (Historical Romance)

Enchanted: 5 Tales of Magic In The Everyday (Children's Book)

<u>Ellis and The Magic Mirror Chapter Book Series (Early Reader)</u>

Ellis and The Magic Mirror

Ellis and The Hidden Cave

Ellis and The Cloud Kingdom